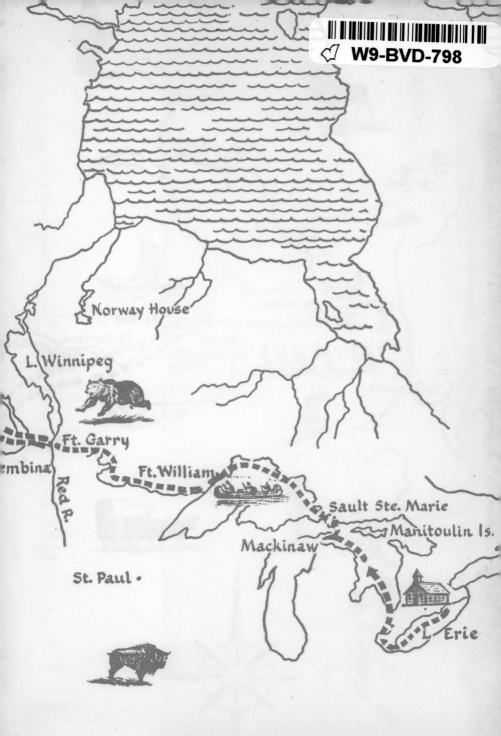

Norway House

L. Winnipeg

Ft. Garry

embina

Red R.

Ft. William

Sault Ste. Marie

Manitoulin Is.

Mackinaw

St. Paul

L. Erie

THE BOY WHO RAN AWAY

THE
BOY
WHO
RAN
AWAY

By JOSEPHINE PHELAN

Illustrated by Vernon Mould

MACMILLAN – TORONTO – 1954

FOR TIMOTHY AND BRIGID

CONTENTS

CONTENTS

1. How It All Began

It was strange that the fight that started him on his travels so quickly faded from his memory. He never thought of it again. Had anyone recalled it to him, he still would have forgotten that he had had the worst of it. But he felt sore and bruised and a little dazed when he came through the woodshed into the kitchen and faced his stepmother over her ironing board.

"Asher Mundy," she cried, "Why are you not at school?"

She was an energetic young woman with a strong ringing voice. He had expected to go through the kitchen unnoticed to his own room. He naturally knew nothing about the afternoons on which there was ironing. With anyone else he might have made excuses, but his stepmother's challenging voice made him sullen and defiant.

"I've been expelled from school," he said. It was true, he had been pulled up by his collar and the back of his jacket and thrown out of the classroom into the corridor. The door had slammed shut with a crack of finality.

Amelia Mundy looked honestly horrified.

"You've been fighting," she said. "You've killed someone!"

"No one's killed. I struck the master. He bullied me."

"Bullied you—you great overgrown thing! Wait till your pa comes home. Your pa will thrash you for this. He'll sure thrash you!"

Her ringing voice had a note of triumph flung after him as he strode through the door leading to the stairs. Goodness knows she had been a careful second wife. She had not interfered between her husband and his firstborn. But Josiah would surely realize now that the boy needed a firm hand. Boys at that age were often unruly. She had wondered lately how soon something would happen that would make her husband realize that he was too easy with the lad.

Upstairs in the room he shared with his brother, Asher Mundy examined himself for damages. There was no mirror so he sat on the bed, blinked his eyes rapidly and felt around them with his fingers. No damage there. He delicately poked his left jaw which was decidedly sore. Then he ground his teeth and poked at them. No blood, nothing loose. He felt some other parts of his anatomy and decided his physical injuries were not serious.

His stepmother's words weighed on his mind heavily. If his father tried to beat him he would strike him, just as he had struck the schoolmaster. No one, *no one*, should lay a hand on him. He was not a child. He found himself shaking with emotion. For months everyone had found fault with him. Even his father found fault. He had become a stranger in his own home. He was becoming a stranger to himself. There was no place for him here any longer. He must go away and find a new life.

Not wishing to face Amelia again he went into the bedroom used by his sisters which had a window overlooking the sloping kitchen roof, which in turn gave onto the lower sloping woodshed roof. Asher raised the window and climbed out. By this easy descent he left the house.

He walked away from the town with its wooden sidewalks and made for the river road where the houses stood far apart, back from the road and the river, with farmland behind them. He knew what he was going to do. His plan did not run very far into the future, but it would settle his difficulties for the moment and to his way of thinking it was wonderfully practical.

He would go to live for a while with Samuel Mott. While everyone else was turning into a stranger, while Asher was becoming a stranger to himself, Sam did not change. Even the idea of going to Sam made him feel more himself. That was because they were both artists, Sam the master and Asher the pupil, cut off from common people by their activities and interests.

Samuel Mott, the artist, was a great bearded man who painted portraits of persons who were important or rich, but who much preferred to paint Indians. He had taught Asher more about painting and drawing than the drawing master at school and he sometimes allowed Asher to call himself his apprentice and work on his canvases.

Sam's house was separated from the road by a creaking gate and an untidy hedge. As Asher went up the path he felt a little uneasy. He had never come to stay like this during school term. But Sam was eccentric and absent-minded and perhaps would notice nothing wrong. Besides, Asher thought he knew how to get round him.

He was amazed at what he found. Sam Mott was closing up his house. Shutters had been closed over the windows even of the rooms he habitually used. His choice Indian paintings were stacked together and covered with dust cloths. On the kitchen floor stood an overstuffed packsack and his gun. His art kit and all sorts of unpacked articles were scattered about.

"Why, Sam," marvelled Asher. "Where are you going?"

"To the North West. To paint Indians."

"Again? After all this time?"

"Much farther this time," said Mott and continued in the frank way in which he sometimes discussed his affairs with the boy. "Beyond the Rocky Mountains to the Pacific country. The Indians there are different from the tribes of the plains. They live in houses and carve immense images of their totems. No one has ever painted them or made a record of their arts."

"Oh, sir," said Asher, and the words came from his very heart. "Take me with you."

Mott gave his great booming laugh. "No, no. That's a journey for men, not boys."

"I am strong and taller than some men. I am of age."

"Are you, indeed? Since when have boys of fifteen years been of age? Why, lad, you must still attend school."

"I am never going to school again. You could take me as your apprentice."

"That's quite impossible," said Mott so flatly that Asher knew he didn't mean it.

He made himself useful. He reminded Mott that he had done nothing about his chickens and went next door to ask the neighbours to look after them. He collected some eggs and made them a supper of fried eggs and potatoes. As they were eating this Asher reopened the conversation.

"When are you leaving, Sam?"

"At six in the morning. The steamer calls on its way to Port Huron."

"I could be ready by then," said Asher calmly, as though going to the North West were all of a piece with putting up shutters and frying eggs.

Sam Mott's eyes began to twinkle. He was fond of this talented, wilful boy.

"What nonsense you are talking. Your father would never permit it."

"Pa has the others," said Asher. "He'll be glad to be rid of me."

"Will he pay your expenses? One does not cross the continent for nothing."

The conversation was reaching a critical point and Asher knew he would have to be careful.

"But I am to be your apprentice. More than once you said I was skilful and that I should be your apprentice. I'm strong and would be very useful on such a journey. Also I can help with the drawings and I can learn."

Sam Mott roared with laughter. "An apprentice worth his weight in gold. And that would be no small sum. Don't talk nonsense; your father would never consent."

"We'll see," said Asher, rising from the table.

There is a tide in the affairs of men which taken at the flood leads on to fortune; omitted, all the voyage of their life is bound in shallows and in miseries. This he had memorized at school from the plays of William Shakespeare. Now he would apply it to his own affairs.

"I am going now," he told Sam. "But I will be back."

He approached his home with the caution of a scout entering enemy country. Standing among the berry bushes, he caught the attention of his two little sisters returning from the outhouse at the end of the garden. It was growing dusk and they screamed in the silly way girls do when he loomed up beside them. But they told him what he wanted to know, that his stepmother was out for the evening attending a church meeting.

In the lordly way he used towards them and without answering their questions, he sent them off to fetch his brother Jonathan, an apt lad of eleven years and very devoted to him. The two boys retired to their bedroom where Asher began some hasty and haphazard packing while he told Jonathan his plans.

"Tell the stepmother I am staying tonight with Samuel Mott. And that's no lie. But say nothing about my going to the North West till pa comes home."

"He'll never let you do it."

"I'll be gone by then. He can't stop me."

"He'll go after you."

"I'll be too far away. Only those with the Company's permission may travel in its territory. Sam knows the Governor."

He rolled together two blankets; dug out his oiled moccasins which he used only in the winter but which he understood were the proper footwear for a *voyageur*; took down the gun that had been a present on his fifteenth birthday. He began packing clothing into his school satchel which had always seemed capacious but now proved too small. Then Jonathan stood before him with a packsack and the buckskin shirt his father wore when he went hunting. He did not say anything, he just held them out to Asher.

"But those are pa's. I couldn't take them."

"You'll need them," said Jonathan.

Conscience waged a short losing fight with necessity. After all this was the last demand he would make on his father. Also time was passing and he must be out of the house before his stepmother returned. He transferred his belongings to the packsack and strapped it on his back. Jonathan insisted on going with him to the end of the street carrying the blanket roll.

"Take me with you," he begged.

"No, no," said Asher with the hard-heartedness of the young. "I'm having trouble getting myself taken. Some time when I'm grown up I'll come back and take you. Good-bye.   Good-bye."

2. The Voyageurs

I

It was still dark when the bearded artist and his runaway apprentice started for the dock. As they made
their way along the road that led down to Lake Erie
the morning dawned, grey and misty, without a sunrise. The steamer docked briefly to pick up two other
passengers besides themselves and some freight.

The more prosperous passengers who had berths were
still abed, but on the lower deck a number of families of
German immigrants were setting out their breakfasts.
Asher watched them for a while. They looked shabby
and worn, like people who had travelled a long way and
not very comfortably. An officious deck hand not much

older than Asher was among them, sweeping the deck
and apparently enjoying ordering them out of his way,
as though he had some authority over them. Another
passenger, leaning against the rail, was also observing
the breakfast scene. He was a rugged-looking fellow in
a faded plaid shirt who might be a lumberjack or even
a *voyageur*. But surely, Asher reminded himself, it was
too soon in their adventure to expect *voyageurs*.

At this point, although he did not realize it, the cabin
boy was addressing him in a strong Cockney accent.

"'Ere, you, move about." Then, prodding him with his
broom, "I say, immigrant, can't you move a bit?"

"Who are you referring to?" asked Asher, towering
to his full height. "Are you looking for trouble, chirper?"

The expression of astonishment on the boy's face was
comical. Asher would have enjoyed the situation if he
had not seen Samuel Mott coming towards him. He
remembered it was less than twenty-four hours since his
last disastrous fight and here he was preparing to start
another one. Fortunately the Cockney boy had other
ideas, and with an "Awh—no offence, to be sure," took
himself off.

"What is your pleasure for breakfast?" asked Mott
good-humouredly. "Do we breakfast with the quality
in the saloon or with common humanity on the lower
deck, out of our own supplies?"

Asher already had had a glimpse of the dining-room
which looked very inviting and did not think too well
of the huddled conditions on the lower deck, but he

doubted that Sam expected a direct answer to his question.

"That is for you to decide, sir," he said politely. "Shall I get something out for us?"

"We'll not have many meals from a cook stove later on; while we're on board we'll use the saloon."

They were the first to arrive for breakfast and Asher surveyed with pleasure the rows of tables covered with stiff white cloths and set out with table napkins folded into peaks and pyramids. Especially was his interest caught by a mural painting of Indians on horses charging across a prairie either in pursuit of an invisible enemy or fleeing from a prairie fire that raged redly in the background.

"What do you think of it?" asked Mott.

"It is magnificent."

"On the contrary. It is bad. I thought, as a result of my instruction, you would have better taste."

"Of course," said Asher judiciously, "the features of the Indians are not well done. They do not have individual expression and character such as you would give them. But there is a great deal to see in this picture and the subject pleases me."

"The artist—or should I call him a sign painter—never saw the scene he depicts. He has never seen an Indian in his native state. He has never seen the prairies. This is copied from a picture, which in turn was probably copied from another picture. Of course it pleases people."

"That is what I mean," said Asher quickly. "It pleases me."

"If you are going to be an artist you will have to have better taste. But for that you must go to Europe and study the works of the great artists. Then you will learn the difference."

Sam Mott had talked like this before. Thank heaven, thought Asher, he says one thing and does another. A studio or gallery in Europe was not to be compared to the fun of going to the North West.

Asher did not see the man who looked like a *voyageur* again until they arrived at Mackinaw, the end of their journey by the steamer. A rustic little port, hemmed in by bush, it greeted the newcomer with the tangy smell of pine and the sight of an Indian encampment. Seen against this background the man in the plaid shirt looked very much at home. Before Asher could begin wondering about him, he made himself known.

"We travel in the same direction, I think, to the North West territory?"

Asher indicated that this was so.

"Bon! I am Napoleon Boucher, a man of good reputation to the Hudson's Bay Company. You have a name?"

The man had an exuberant and winning manner. His eyes sparkled and his smile disclosed dazzling white teeth. He spoke with a strong French accent and depended on gesture and facial expression as much as on words to convey his meaning. Indeed Asher hardly knew which made the most sense and found himself using the same means to carry on the conversation. He gave his name and Napoleon tried it out delightedly.

"Ashair! Then we travel together—yes? You look for the brigade, too?"

This was moving too fast for Asher. He had often heard his father, speaking from his experience in publishing a weekly newspaper, say that one should always be careful in dealing with pleasant-spoken strangers as they sometimes proved the worst rascals.

"I am travelling with a gentleman who is going into Rupert's Land to paint Indians. He is an artist and has been there before."

"Ah-ha," commented Napoleon as though this was just the piece of information he had been looking for. "The big barbe," he made a full gesture of his hand beneath his chin, "you travel with him. So! I go now to address myself to him."

He looked at the pile of luggage which Asher had been left to watch. "The world is not an honest place, heh?" Then with a gesture to his own gear and to Asher that could not be mistaken he said: "Gardez ces choses-là." And set off to look for Mott.

Asher was left to fume at the unheroic position in which he found himself, until presently his artist friend joined him. He and Napoleon Boucher had talked in French, in which language Mott was proficient, and quickly arrived at an understanding. They must, as soon as possible, attach themselves to a brigade of Company cargo canoes going to Fort Garry. Napoleon's suggestion was that they should travel together as far as

Fort Sault Ste. Marie, the point of departure for the brigades. Napoleon hoped to be taken on, as he was a *voyageur* who had worked for the Company before. He said he had *"affaires"* in Mackinaw, though just what the *"affaires"* were he had not explained, and that he owned a canoe which they could use to take them to Fort Sault Ste. Marie, as the steamer service from this point was irregular.

"Do you think he is a sound man?" asked Asher in some concern.

"I don't doubt he's honest, if a little boastful. We'll go and have a look at his canoe."

"But what about the baggage?" asked the conscientious Asher. So Sam Mott offered to look after it and sent Asher down to the shore to a group of ramshackle boathouses. There he found Napoleon looking at his canoe. It was a big travel-stained birch canoe, bigger than those Asher was accustomed to. Napoleon carried it to the end of a low dock and slid it into the water where it landed with a flat-sounding plop and rode light as a leaf. While Asher held it to the dockside Napoleon tossed in paddles and a few pieces of gear. Then they set off to join Mott.

Now that he had secured his companions, Napoleon was less talkative. His mind was on the expedition. He barked a few directions at Asher which suggested that Sam Mott was not going to be his only instructor. Once he asked: "The old man, how is he for the paddle?"

"Oh, very good," said Asher promptly. He could not imagine Sam undertaking anything he could not accomplish.

"For you it is the first voyage," said Napoleon, encouragingly. "But you will learn."

For three days they toiled through the tangle of islands and waterways that led from Manitoulin to the mouth of the St. Mary's River. Napoleon reminded them more than once: "This is the time the brigades leave. If we miss the brigades we are finished." He drove them mercilessly and worked himself like three men, or so he said. He tried to cheer them along with song in the *voyageur* manner, but even he was not able to sing with the volume and harmony of three men. Asher would willingly have learned the songs, French words and all, but his singing was not successful.

"At your age," said Napoleon regretfully, "the voice is not good."

Sam Mott did not care to sing. He shared the *voyageur's* sense of urgency. When Asher suggested that they should sketch some of the scenes of their travel, he replied that this was not even the entrance to the country they were setting out to visit. This was nothing. His mind leapt ahead to that country, for he spoke sometimes of the bold, magnificent Indians of the far western prairies, and even oftener of the tribes beyond the Rocky Mountains that they were going to see for the first time. They were entirely different from the tribes of the plains, he had heard, and possessed a strange, intricate art, carving their family histories on totem poles. He asked Napoleon Boucher what he knew of these tribes. But Napoleon had never been beyond the mountains.

Asher alone enjoyed the voyage for itself. Hardly an hour passed that his eyes did not rest on some scene of beauty that he could imagine forming a splendid background for Sam Mott's Indians. At night, rolled in their blankets against the cold, they slept on windy, rocky promontories to avoid the black flies. Before sun-up they had eaten their breakfast and were launching their canoe for another day's travel.

II

In this fashion they came to Sault Ste. Marie, the first fort of the Hudson's Bay Company on their journey. Asher marvelled at the size of the great canoes capable of carrying twenty-six men or, with a small crew, hundreds of pounds of cargo. And yet these canoes in themselves were almost as light as Napoleon Boucher's smaller craft. Three of these canoes were being filled with *voyageurs* who departed through the lock that raised them to the head of the rapids down which the river ran fiercely at this point.

On their arrival Mott and his companions found the post alive with *voyageurs*. Within an hour it was almost deserted. With growing dismay and disappointment both Sam Mott and Napoleon appealed to the factor to find them places in the outgoing canoes. With the best will in the world the factor could do nothing for them.

"Your best plan," he said, "is to continue on to Fort William. The Governor himself is there at this moment. If you can reach him before he leaves for Fort Garry, and since, Mr. Mott, you say he has given you com-

missions before, I am sure he will arrange for your transportation."

But how were they to reach Fort William? It was one
thing for three men to paddle a medium-sized canoe
through the comparatively sheltered channels approaching the Sault, but quite another thing to follow the big,
fully-manned, cargo canoes along miles of the exposed
shoreline of Lake Superior. Even Napoleon Boucher
with the strength of three men knew he dared not
attempt this with his untrained crew.

The factor, willing to be helpful, said that the Company's schooner was loading with large supplies for
Fort William and would leave in a few days. It would
almost certainly overtake the brigade before it left Fort
William.

It was the best arrangement they could make. Napoleon Boucher accepted it on condition that his canoe
should go with them. It might be that they would miss
the brigade and have to pursue it up the river, where
its route lay, to its first portage.

"The brigades travel fast," he said. "And Sir George
Simpson—" he made a great gesture—"he goes like the
wind."

The factor hired Napoleon to help with the loading
of the schooner and might even have offered Asher a
job but, in the way boys have when there is work to be
done, that young man had disappeared. He was later
seen sketching the fort from a position below the rapids.

Accuracy and clearness of detail were important because Sam Mott's purpose was to make a pictorial record

of a new country in the days before photography provided a quicker method. But Samuel Mott also believed
in the artist's eye that picked out what was essential
and to be emphasized. Asher remembered his master's
teachings as he worked over his drawing of the little
trading post.

Sam Mott looked at the sketch when Asher brought
it to him and secretly found it praiseworthy. But as he
believed that praise stopped progress he was cautious
about expressing approval.

"If this is intended as a background for a portrait
your composition is poor. You have filled in the fore-
ground. Where am I to place the figure?"

"I only wanted to make a sketch of what I saw. If
we were in the Indian country and you were painting
people of course I would plan the picture differently."

Sam flipped through the pages and turned up a sketch
of the rapids.

"This is too ambitious a subject for you."

Asher reddened a little. "I did not mean you to see
it. I was just trying."

"You are not wrong to be ambitious," said Mott slowly. "But soon you will need a different kind of teaching."

Why had he brought the boy on a hare-brained journey into wild country when even now he was ready for
the studios of Europe? Then he remembered that this
had not been planned at all. Asher had attached himself to the expedition by some means that was not quite
clear.

They arrived at Fort William on a brisk clear morning and found the river front aswarm with *voyageurs.* How quick they were, swinging packs from one to another, stowing them neatly away in the canoes as though they worked to music. Sam Mott and his party were told that Sir George Simpson was at the mess hall with his staff but would travel ahead of the brigade.

Napoleon Boucher spoke to Mott in French: "M'sieu, you will not forget me when you are talking to Sir George. I have travelled with the brigades and the agents know I am a good man. But the Governor—you see it is not like that for me. Speak for me and perhaps we can continue to travel in the same party."

Mott assured him he would do what he could. Then he and Asher set out for the mess hall, built by the North West Company in the pride of its might when it had competed with the great Hudson's Bay Company itself for the fur empire. For many years the two companies had been joined and Fort William was no longer the headquarters. But the Hudson's Bay Company still gave importance to the fort and when the Governor visited it he used the mess hall where his predecessors had held large and riotous entertainments.

Sam Mott told Asher that the hall was very fine inside and that among its treasures were several of his paintings, ordered by the Company on his first visit to the North West.

As they entered the huge raftered dining-hall they met Sir George. He came towards them down the length of the hall accompanied by his secretary, the factor and several other official persons with whom he had just finished an early dinner. He was a little under average height and was dressed very correctly like a business man who was going to his office in the city rather than setting out for hundreds of miles of travel in a canoe.

When he saw the big bearded artist and the tall boy waiting to speak to him he hesitated very slightly, holding up his hand as though to prevent Mott from speaking first.

"I know who you are," he said. "Samuel Mott, the artist who paints Indians."

"You have a good memory, Sir George," replied Mott smiling.

"Where are you off to now? To paint more Indians?"

"This time I hope to go beyond the Rockies to study the tribes of the Pacific."

"And what can I do for you?" asked the Governor who did not waste words.

"This boy and I would like passage with the brigade going to Fort Garry. There is a *voyageur* also, Napoleon Boucher, who has been most useful in getting us this far. He also would like to go to the Red River country with the brigade."

The Governor turned to his secretary.

"Masterman, see that Mr. Mott receives a letter over my name addressed to the factors requesting every courtesy for him and his party. Mr. McTavish," said Sir George to the factor, "will you have the kindness to see that there are places in the brigade for the party, and for the *voyageur*, Napoleon Boucher, also. Who is this lad?" he asked Mott.

"Asher Mundy," replied the artist. "My student, or you might say my apprentice. We artists must have our apprentices too, Sir George."

"How old are you, lad?" the Governor asked Asher.

"Twenty, sir," replied Asher pulling himself up to his full height.

Sir George looked surprised. "You are a tall lad but I would have thought that you were younger. You are not kidnapping him, are you?" he said good-naturedly to Mott. Then he took his leave as quickly as he had greeted them. "I am sorry that I cannot invite you to travel with our party, but we travel light. Good luck, Mr. Mott, in your enterprise."

Sir George and his officials left the building; and Asher and his friend almost directly after them without lingering to look at the paintings as he had expected.

"Why did you lie to him?" Mott asked furiously. Asher had never seen him so angry.

"I—I don't know," he stammered. "It seemed better to appear older."

"It was stupid and unmanly," declared Mott.

Asher felt abashed. He had not thought of his deception as a lie but as a kind of disguise proper to the adventure they were undertaking.

"I supposed you lied to me too about having your father's permission."

"I have not lied to you, Sam Mott. I told you that my father was not at home. That I left word with my stepmother and a message for my father."

Mott in his moment of anger would have liked to tell Asher that if he had not lied to him he had certainly deceived him. But even in anger he was a fair-minded man. He knew he had wanted to bring the boy with him and had allowed himself to be deceived.

He left Asher severely to himself while he went to get his letter from the secretary and consult McTavish about the transportation.

"I have drawn up papers," he told Asher on his return, "that make you my heir in the event of my death, and my ward for the duration of this journey."

Asher was astonished. Indeed, he was not quite sure what Sam meant, except that it sounded as though he was going to act like a parent, and that would be a bad thing! But Sam did not seem in a mood to answer questions so Asher did not ask them.

Sir George Simpson left Fort William, ceremoniously preceded to his canoe by his Scottish piper playing the bagpipes, a sight that never failed to impress the *voyageurs* and the simple inhabitants of the Company's forts.

Asher too was impressed by the piper, but Sir George in his broadcloth coat and tall black hat looked to him like any business man dressed for church on Sunday. He was glad that they were not travelling with his party but with the *voyageurs*.

He did not know that Sir George and the great Company would soon be mixed up in his affairs in a fashion that would bring satisfaction to nobody. Already Josiah

Mundy, filled with grief and anxiety at the loss of his son, had consulted a lawyer and on his advice had sent letters to all the known trading posts of the Hudson's Bay Company asking the help of the Governor and the Company in finding and returning to him his son, Asher Mundy, a minor, who had been kidnapped and carried off to the North West by one Samuel Mott, an artist of eccentric and irresponsible behaviour.

III

For ten days the brigade climbed, if it could be said to climb by water. The big canoes forced their way against the current. When the river cascaded down stone terraces to meet them, the crews portaged, carrying canoes and freight up the river to the next stretch of smooth water.

Asher took his place at the paddle, but as he and Mott were passengers they were not expected to carry the ninety-pound loads. They had their own baggage to see to. Asher added the art supplies to his load and, imitating the *voyageurs*, balanced the whole on his back with the aid of a tumpline supporting the pack and braced against the forehead.

The *voyageurs* at first were inclined to make fun of him because he could not speak their language and they could not speak his. Here Napoleon Boucher proved a powerful friend.

Let them not think too highly of themselves, he warned them. Fellows who travelled between Lachine and Fort Garry in the summer-time and had never spent a winter on the plains. Asher Mundy would be a true *voyageur* before any of them. Dreadful sounding names he called them—*mangeurs de lard, soupes aux pois*—and all in a good-natured way. Even the names, as Asher soon learned, were not so dreadful—pork-eaters and pea soups. A true *voyageur* ate pemmican.

"But you don't eat pemmican," argued Asher.

"Ah, but I *have* eaten pemmican. And M'sieu Mott, he has eaten pemmican. Don't you see that we are different." And he roared with laughter.

Asher thought Sam Mott and Napoleon different from anyone he had ever met, but he did not know if he was supposed to take Napoleon seriously.

At last they crossed the height of land and the rivers began to flow with them instead of against them. Sometimes they ran the rapids instead of portaging. Asher, sitting tense in his place in the big canoe, found that it was all over very quickly, really it seemed nothing at all, except for those few wildly exciting minutes when they slid through the swift, glassy-smooth water into the foaming, churning stretch of white water that broke over the rocks. He would willingly have run every rapid they passed, even those too dangerous to attempt. Reckless themselves, the *voyageurs* liked his recklessness. He began to win their approval.

The crews sang oftener and more cheerfully now, keeping time with their paddles. They sang old French songs that had been sung for so long that no one remembered when they had begun. Some of them must have been as old as the hills, although not as old as the hills through which they were travelling. They were Laurentian rock, the oldest hills in the world.

On the rare occasions when the brigade made camp early Sam Mott and Asher got out their sketching boards. Their sketches impressed the *voyageurs* and Napoleon Boucher was as proud of them as if he had made them himself. Occasionally Indians came to their camp bringing fresh fish which they bought to vary their dull fare of salt pork. But most of the time they camped at dusk and met no one.

It was a wild, beautiful country, but lonely and strange. Perhaps if they could have lingered in camp, gone fishing or gone into the woods to hunt, the country would not have seemed so lonely and unfriendly. But Sir George Simpson and his party were ahead in their swift canoe. The brigade must not lag too far behind. The traders in charge of the canoes had their orders and the *voyageurs* also took pride in making good time. It was a game, with records to be made and broken.

Sam Mott warned Asher never to leave the water's edge when they were in camp.

"In half an hour you could be hopelessly lost in that bush and, frankly, I don't think the brigade would wait to look for you."

Some of the phrases in the *voyageurs'* speech were beginning to have meaning for Asher. He understood *"le pays d'en haut"* meant the far country and it was the one they were going to, not the country they were passing through. This was their road, but the far country was their goal.

They followed the rivers in a great arc north and then swung south into Lake Winnipeg, a body of water fully as vast as Lake Erie on which Asher had his home. Here the *voyageurs* rigged their canoes with square sails and slipped lazily before the wind when it was favourable. But this good time did not last long. When they entered the Red River they had to bend again to their paddles, for the current flowed strongly against them.

Then the weather turned against them too, driving wind and rain, rain beating down on them hour after hour like showers of watery arrows. Instead of making a grand entry into Fort Garry in gay costume and full song they arrived at the lower Stone Fort beaten and sodden, more like refugees than conquering *voyageurs*.

3. The Buffalo Hunters

I

ASHER MUNDY stood on the bank of the Red River and looked north and south at its dark, muddied waters, up and down its steep muddy banks, across at the prairie steaming from the rain under a dull sky. So this was the *pays d'en haut*, the far country. He had never imagined there could be so much mud, so many puddles anywhere. What scenery was there to paint here? Mud, just mud. A horrible country! Sam Mott and Napoleon Boucher must be crazy to think well of it. He could understand why the *mangeurs de lard* did not remain, but as soon as they could returned with the brigades to Montreal.

Sam Mott was buying equipment, a two-wheeled Red River cart that screeched hideously on its wooden axles.

He was hesitating between a horse and an ox to draw it. An *ox* in a country where everyone rode horseback!

"If only we could have horses to *ride*," Asher burst out bitterly. "Not one old nag or an old *cow!*"

He had to stop because he was actually on the point of tears. It was childish and it was not the way to deal with Sam, but he could not help himself. Sam Mott, surprisingly patient, made no reply. But soon after he began bargaining for a good little prairie horse, so that in the end their travelling outfit was made up of the creaking Red River cart to carry their tent and baggage, one horse to draw the cart and a better one which they would take turns riding.

They were to travel alone. It was hard to know about Sam Mott. Sometimes he behaved like a rich man, sometimes he was sparing. Now he said he could not afford a guide. He expected to find Metis hunters on the prairie. Among them he would find some one to act as interpreter when they met the Indians.

They set out under a gentle blue sky, Sam Mott driving the cart and Asher riding the horse. They drove over prairie unmarked by roads but criss-crossed by half-covered ruts of former carts. A rolling country dotted with clumps of trees that marked the river courses and the prairie sloughs. Among these they camped at night so as to have water and wood for their fire.

Sam Mott liked a story before going to sleep and had Asher read to him from a limp-bound Bible.

"It's full of rare stories," he told Asher. "Best story book in the world."

Nothing Sam Mott did surprised Asher, though he had never thought of him as a church-going man. He was, however, a little shocked to hear Mott refer to the sacred book as a story book. But he did not object to the suggestion that he choose what he liked. He chose the livelier stories, full of action, David and Goliath, Daniel in the lions' den, and grew quick at riffling through the pages till he found a new one.

After the lantern was put out he plunged into sleep as into a pool, eager to be through the night and start another day.

All about them the prairie grass was gay with flowers and once they drove through an endless stretch of wild roses that tossed lightly in the breeze, scattering their delicate perfume. It was a land that surely belonged to the morning of the world.

"It's a fine country," said Asher.

"Aha," commented Sam Mott. "I thought you would come to like it."

Asher, cantering off from the lumbering, creaking cart, rode through the field of roses like a prince.

It was this habit of cantering off on his own that brought him to disaster. He found himself in swampy land, crossed by little streams, and the little hillocks that should have marked the edge of the swamp only led him in deeper. He turned his horse this way and that, quite sure that he had not come far from the open prairie. The swamp seemed to have moved in round him. Mosquitoes

swarmed about him, stinging and confusing him   He
called out loudly, but only the wild fowl rose up flapping
their wings and startling his horse.

The animal shied, throwing its rider, then plunged off
skittishly, while he scrambled after it. He found himself
floundering up to his knees in mud and water. Horrible
stories of quicksand came to him and he screamed out
again. He feared he would lose sight of the horse, his
last hope. It stopped a little distance off, rolling a bright
eye at him, as though it thought him a fool.

He splashed up out of the hole, seized the trailing
bridle and remounted, while clouds of mosquitoes nearly blinded him. Once again on his horse he tried to follow the course of one of the streams on the theory that
a stream like a road must lead somewhere. It only led
him into a deeper, wider stretch of swamp water. Now
his horse floundered about and finally stopped dead
and refused to move in any direction.

Shuddering at the thought of sinking again into the
swamp water, Asher forced himself to dismount and,
wading up to his waist in slime and mud, made for the
bunches of tough, matted grass that grew above the
water level. He held tightly to the long lariat attached
to the horse's neck and when he reached firmer, if not
drier, ground he pulled and urged until the horse splashed up beside him.

Again he mounted and unfastened a blanket, wrap-
ping it about him to keep out the tormenting mosquitoes.
But they were inside his clothes, in his ears, everywhere.
If it had not been for the insects he might have been

able to think. But they maddened him, giving him no rest.

This kept up all day.

Finally the boy gave up, clinging to his horse, sobbing and gasping. The animal, wiser than its rider, now that it was no longer driven this way and that, picked its way carefully through the morass and at last came out on firm ground.

Here the horse and its dazed rider were discovered by a young half-breed scout and brought to a camp of Metis hunters nearby.

II

The Metis were on their annual buffalo hunt and travelled in full force with their women, children, dogs and horses. Their tepees, arranged in orderly converging circles, made a small village. That day they had made their first buffalo run and most of them were now busy skinning and dividing enough of the carcases to supply meat for the whole camp. The Metis like other prairie people travelled light; supplies had run low and everyone was hungry. They were all taking the liveliest interest in the preparations.

To Asher Mundy it was a scene of horror. The great carcases of the buffaloes, some half stripped of their hides, the exposed muscles and tendons streaked with blood, the hacking and quartering, the piles of torn out entrails, the carefully set aside delicacies, tongues and humps—no butcher shop could have prepared him for this grisly sight. And everyone seemed to be enjoying himself.

His young guide brought him to his family's tepee and gave him water to drink (he was agonized by thirst) and also ointment to rub on his face and neck which were spotted with blood from the insect bites and beginning to swell and itch. Asher in his own way was as gruesome a sight as the butchered buffalo.

"We'll eat soon," said his guide cheerfully. "And then you'll feel better."

Already meat was being expertly roasted before well-banked fires. The smell of it was very agreeable. When Asher was offered a portion on a wooden platter he set to with the appetite of fatigue.

Then the first wave of nausea hit him. He hastily withdrew from the group of feasters and was violently ill. Some time later—he soon lost track of time and place—someone in pity led him to a make-shift bed in a tepee.

He passed the night in violent spasms of retching, longing for death. Towards morning, apparently having vomited up his very bowels, he sank into a sleep of utter exhaustion.

When he woke a dark Metis woman brought him a basin of water, soap and a towel. She told him to take off his fouled shirt and provided him with a fresh one. She gave him ointment to relieve the intolerable itching of the mosquito bites. Then she brought him a steaming bowl of broth and told him to drink it. He shrank from it, but again she told him to drink it. So he took it down. It didn't taste bad.

Most of the words the woman used were French and Asher understood some, but not all of them. However, he thought it would not be hard to understand anyone so kind and sensible, no matter what language she spoke. He leaned back weakly on his bed, glad to be alive.

The woman squatted on the ground beside him with the ease of one who has never bothered much with chairs.

"Where do you come from?" she asked.

He told her Upper Canada, but she looked puzzled. In phrases he remembered from the *voyageurs* he added: "Loin. Pays d'en haut." This she seemed to understand.

"Have you any parents," she asked, "or any friends?"

"My mother is dead," answered Asher. Then recalling the French he had learned from the *voyageurs,* he ventured into her own language. "Ma mère est morte et mon père ne m'aime pas. (And my father doesn't like me.)"

The woman gave an expression of sympathy and Asher himself believed he had never put the situation more touchingly. The woman rose and the conversation was over.

"Bon!" she said briskly with a clap of her hands. "Lève-toi."

Asher was shocked. Surely she didn't mean him to get up in his weakened condition. But that apparently was just what she meant and Asher thought it best to obey her.

He rose shakily and went to the opening of the tent where a beautiful morning greeted him and also Angus Ouellette, the boy who had rescued him.

"Good morning," said Angus in English. "How are you?"

The subject was almost too vast for Asher to consider.

"I almost died last night," he said.

"It is the gnat bites. They are poisonous for strangers," said Angus. "Let's go and look at the horses."

"What am I to do about my friend, Mr. Mott? I'm afraid he's lost."

"You are the one lost," Angus pointed out. "But our scouts are looking for your party. We are well organized here."

They found their horses with the others just beyond the camp. Angus had brought a brush and a curry comb. He began grooming his mount.

"We take care of our horses at the fort. Many of these are neglected."

"Why do you speak English?" asked Asher. "No one else does here?"

"You find I speak well?" said Angus with pleasure. "At the fort I took lessons with the factor's son. The doctor gave us lessons; there is no school at the fort. But now I think maybe I go away to school—to Montreal."

Asher considered this doubtfully.

"Aren't you too old for that if you have never been to school before?"

"I think of that too," admitted Angus.

"I wouldn't go if I were you," Asher advised him. "I have been to school and I assure you, you won't like it."

"Perhaps I'll find that out also," said Angus.

"Who looked after me this morning?"

"She is my mother."

Asher insisted on getting the name correctly and repeated it after Angus.

"Ouellette. Madame Ouellette. Mama Ouellette."

Sam Mott and his Red River cart arrived in camp that day, brought in by the scouts. He was inclined to blame Asher for getting lost.

"Why didn't you fire off your gun?" he asked. And Asher felt so foolish not to have thought of this that he couldn't find anything to answer.

Mott stayed another day at the Metis camp collecting some more supplies and trading the cart horse for a better one. The Metis were preparing to march again, but their pace, impeded by baggage and families, was too ponderously slow for Sam. To Asher's plea that they remain with the Metis at least until after another buffalo hunt, he replied that he had come to paint buffaloes not to hunt them.

"Also," he added, "I am looking for Indians, not half-breeds, even though there are some fine-looking fellows among them."

III

"I cannot draw this country," complained Asher as he sat with his sketch book outside their tent early in the evening of their first night out from the Metis camp. "All sky and horizon—if I were using paints—all the colour —but it isn't colour, it's light. You can't paint light."

"Don't be discouraged," replied Sam. "This is not the time to set up canvas and prepare paints. When we come to the mountains you'll have plenty of scenery, and when the light falls on those fields of snow and masses of rock the colours are solid seeming."

"When do you think we'll arrive there? What about the Pacific Ocean and the tribes of the coast? Aren't they the ones we started out to find?"

"One thing at a time, impatient. We'll spend the summer in the foothills of the Rockies among the Blackfoot Indians. Then we'll join a Company brigade passing through the mountains and spend the winter on the Pacific coast. How is that?"

Asher was silent some time considering this agreeable prospect. Then he fearfully made a request that he had more than once hinted at.

"Sam, will you teach me to draw figures and faces?"

"No. You will have to go elsewhere to learn that."

"But Sam, you are an excellent portrait painter. Why do you refuse me?"

"I have been well taught, but I am not equipped to teach others."

Sam Mott, wearing steel-rimmed spectacles, was making an entry in his diary. Now he closed the book and removed the spectacles with the schoolmasterly air of beginning an explanation.

"You will learn some day, or I hope you will learn, what is involved. You will begin with a skeleton and study the bones. You will study all the joints and all the angles of the joints. The muscles and their contractions. The tissues of the skin layer by layer. There will come a time when you will wonder if you are a medical student rather than an artist. But in the end you will be able to paint the portrait of a man and show his character with every stroke of your brush. You will be able to paint the face of a woman and show the glance of pride or the look of love."

As they drove westward the next day Sam pointed to a buffalo skull lying in their path.

"There is your first lesson if you wish. Observe the skulls of buffaloes when you see them. Then try to supply what lies between the skull and the outer head of the living animal. Observe and draw if you will the joints and muscles of your horse. But do not practice on the Blackfoot Indians when we meet them. They are a proud people and very critical of portraiture—as I know from having been among them. They regard an artist as a kind of medicine man and if your efforts were clumsy they would regard them as bad medicine. They are dangerous if offended."

"Are they really cruel as people say? Torturing prisoners and burning at the stake and all that?"

"They are cruel to their enemies in warfare," said Mott shortly. "But we go among them as friends. The older men of the tribe are often persons of great dignity."

After his misadventure in the swamp Asher was more careful. He had learned painfully the treachery of the country and he never fully trusted it again. Even so disaster again fell on the little expedition.

It began with bad weather, driving rain such as had greeted them when they first came into the country.

Their horses forged ahead slowly over the sodden prairie, heads lowered against the wind. At night they camped in dampness and misery.

The third day Sam Mott took a chill. The weather began to clear, but their troubles continued. Sam was racked by a painful cough and fever. He insisted that they push on, in his illness feeling more need for company than was his habit. Even an Indian encampment would have some remedies. Asher thought they should turn back to the Metis.

As it happened they had to camp where they were, as Sam was too ill to travel. Asher pitched the tent successfully, made a good fire and spread out their blankets to dry. Then he used the saddle and blankets to make his friend a fairly comfortable bed.

Pneumonia. Neither of them had ever used or heard the word. But when Mott between painful bouts of gasping for breath whispered, "inflammation of the lungs," Asher felt his heart like an icy fist in his chest. His mother had died of "inflammation of the lungs."

"It can be fought," Sam gasped slowly, but resolutely. He instructed Asher to bring out a bottle of whiskey and give him small doses at intervals.

All that day, timing himself with Sam's gold watch, Asher gave the sick man the liquor every hour and a half. He had no idea whether or not it was the right remedy, but Sam seemed easier. He was stubbornly and cautiously fighting the disease with all his reserves of strength. He said, carefully gathering breath for each phrase: "There will be a crisis. Then a sweat. And the fever will leave me."

As evening came Asher read a little to him, hoping it might lull him to sleep. His rugged favourites from the Old Testament hardly seemed suitable for the purpose so he chose a New Testament parable.

"A certain man went down from Jerusalem to Jericho and fell among thieves, which stripped him of his raiment and wounded him, and departed, leaving him half dead." When the good Samaritan came into the story Asher thought of the Metis woman, Mama Ouellette, and wished they were both safely under her care. Presently Sam slept and he dozed.

He was wakened by the sick man threshing about in delirium. He brought him water to ease his fever and sat by him helplessly.

Next day the patient seemed oddly quiet. Asher hoped the crisis had passed; the fever seemed gone. But his instinct, wiser than his hope, warned him all was not well. Sam seemed to have withdrawn to a distance and he no longer fought his illness. Towards evening he roused himself a little and bit by bit, but quite distinctly, said: "When this is over—you go home—there is a will—enough for Europe—Italy is best."

Asher lifted him a little, trying by a change in position to ease his breathing.

"Sam," he said slowly, "don't give up. Hold on a while longer. Sam, don't leave me here alone."

It was nearly midnight when Sam Mott died.

Asher, frantically looking for he knew not what remedy, turned and saw that his friend was beyond need.
He covered his face and sat on the ground beside him,
too numb for tears. Exhausted by his long watching he
finally fell asleep. The living and the dead lay side by
side during the night.

In the morning he sprang up, horrified at what he had
done. He went to the opening of the tent and looked
at the prairie, ashimmer with gold haze in the early
morning light, utterly beautiful. The two horses wandered at a little distance. It was a peaceful scene, miles
and miles of lovely country and nowhere another living human creature.

Asher Mundy was quite alone and had to make all the
decisions. He could not bear to think of burying his
friend without someone by him. So he decided to turn
back and to allow two days to find the Metis hunters.

In the midst of his heavy troubles he had a bit of luck.
The first day he met with a scout from the Metis camp,
a Cree-Metis who spoke neither French nor English. But
he brought him to the camp and to the Ouellette family.

The Metis leaders regretted that they had no priest
with them. Asher pointed out that Sam Mott was a
Protestant so that a Catholic funeral might not be in
order. But the hunters were certain that had their chaplain been with them he would have arranged something
appropriate.

Lacking this, they dug a grave for him on the prairie.
The assembled camp sang hymns that had in their rhy-

thm the long sweep of the canoe paddle. Then Asher
was invited to take his part. He read a passage from
the Scriptures, too dazed with grief to remember afterwards which one he had chosen. The Metis listened res-
pectfully though they did not understand the language.
The grave was closed and the hunters fired a ragged
volley over it. Then the women and older children
built a cairn of stones and Asher set up a wooden plaque
carved with his friend's name and the date of his death;
he did not know when he had been born.

Such was the death and burial of Samuel Mott, the
artist who painted Indians.

IV

Asher found he was now a person of some importance.
He was the sole survivor of the tiny expedition and the
heir to Sam Mott's belongings, the two horses, the Red
River cart, his gun, his gold watch, all his personal goods.

The women who had made the simple preparations of
the body for burial brought Asher the money belt, the
letter from Sir George Simpson and a few other items
they had found on it. Among none of these things did
he find a copy of the will Mott had spoken of.

He looked through the diary. The entries were brief,
the date and a line or two for each day. Turning to the
day they had spent at Fort William he found a short
entry. "Made will. Asher Mundy my heir." The six
words told him all he needed to know.

In the money belt he found nearly three hundred
dollars in bank bills. There were also some gold and

silver coins, each curiously encircled in a little frame of soft metal, complete with a loop through which a cord could pass. Asher puzzled over these and decided that Sam had intended to use them in trade with the Indians and had made them so that they could be used as ornaments. How like Sam, in some ways so saving, to use real coins instead of the shiny trash usually given to the savages! Seeing these intimate things brought Sam Mott back vividly. The hard knot of grief loosened and for the first time since his friend's death, Asher wept unashamedly and bitterly.

It seemed suitable that he should attach himself to the Ouellette family. At night he slept beside Angus and rode beside him on the slow daily march. When it was the turn of Cyprian Ouellette to be the leader for the day, Asher rode in the vanguard with Angus and his father, the camp flag fluttering over them. At such times life seemed pretty good to Asher Mundy.

Scouts brought in news that a herd of bison grazed some miles ahead and the whole expedition was thrown into orderly excitement. The women and older children promptly started pitching camp. The best horses, the buffalo runners, were led out. The men who were going to make the run began examining their weapons and harness, priming their muzzle-loaders, tightening saddle girths, as though a buffalo hunter did not always keep his gear in readiness.

The Metis like their Indian cousins were buffalo people and, since their white blood prevented them from going on the war-path, Indian fashion, the buffalo hunt was the greatest event in their lives.

Asher made his preparations, watching Angus to be sure he did the right thing. When everyone was ready the hunters started off with the scouts in the direction of the herd, riding slowly so as to save their horses.

"I have never seen a buffalo," said Asher, then regretted his remark. He might be thought too inexperienced for the hunt. But Angus only said:

"Have you no buffalo in your country? I learnt that before, but it is hard for me to believe it."

Now that Asher had lived in the Metis camp he could understand how that could be. The Metis built their tepees of buffalo skin and covered their beds with buffalo robes. They made clothing and moccasins of buffalo hide. They ate buffalo meat and made it into pemmican for winter use and for sale to the Hudson's Bay Company.

How begin to explain to Angus that in his country tents were made of canvas and bedding consisted of quilts and blankets, clothes were made from cotton, woollen and silk and for meat they ate beef, lamb and pork.

"Do you have horses in your country?" asked Angus.

"Oh, certainly, and our carriages have four wheels. We also have other amazing things like steamboats." Asher described the lake steamer he had travelled on.

"If I go to Montreal," said Angus, "maybe I will see steamboats. Do you think I might travel on one?"

"Yes, I suppose you might," admitted Asher reluctantly. He did not like to hear Angus talk about leaving Rupert's Land.

"Oh look, Angus," he cried. "There are the buffalo."

As they came to the top of a gently rising hill they saw about a quarter of a mile away the plain alive with the grazing bison. Even at this distance Asher could see their outlines clearly, great head, chest and shoulders, dainty little legs and narrow hind quarters. Surely among the strangest-looking animals developed by nature.

The hunters halted and gathered about Cyprian who assigned their places and gave the well-known orders for the hunt. It was conducted as a rough sort of military operation.

The Metis hunters formed a long, slightly curving line. Angus and Asher as inexperienced boys were assigned positions well towards one end. The line moved forward slowly towards the herd. The plan was to come as close as possible before charging. The horses, as keen for the hunt as their riders, were restive and quivering with excitement, but the hunters sat them confident and steady as centaurs.

Asher's horse catching the excitement from the others reared and plunged. Angus stretched out his arm and laid a steadying hand on the bridle. They rode forward side by side. Closer and closer they came to the herd, approaching it from the leeward because, while the buffalo's sight was poor, its sense of smell was acute.

The horses were gradually trotting faster as they advanced. Then one and then another bull sensed danger, tossed its head and began to paw the ground.

"En avant!" Cyprian Ouellette's voice rang out clear and sharp.

"Ho! Ho!" came back the hunting cry of the Metis as the horses, released, charged forward in a whirlwind of dust. The quiet of a minute before was broken by the thunder of hooves, a thunder that grew deeper as the herd began to stampede.

The two boys were carried along on a wave of exhilaration over uneven ground full of badger holes. Near him Asher saw a horse stumble and the rider pitch forward over its head. Asher pulled sharply on his reins, but his horse, paying not the slightest attention charged on. Panic swept over him when he realized the horse was running away with him. With long leaps and short leaps, the prairie pony bounded over the uneven dangerous ground at a mad pace. Asher had never ridden like this. He gripped the animal's flanks tightly with his knees and twisted his fingers into its mane, determined to hang on come what may. It was the same wise little horse that had brought him out of the swamp. He had blind confidence in it and in Angus who galloped beside him.

The situation became a little easier. Those in the centre of the line had been swept right into the stampeding herd. But Angus and Asher out towards the end were in a less dangerous position.

A great bull buffalo, broken away from the herd, came charging toward them. The buffalo swerved this way and that, peering fiercely with its little red eyes, while the excited horses and their riders pranced about it.

"Garde!" cried Angus, to remind his friend to beware of bullets. Having circled the animal he rode down on it from the front, aimed his gun, firing at close range, and neatly planted a bullet in a vulnerable spot near the eye.

The animal halted, stood rock solid with its legs apart, as though it knew this was its last stand. Asher could have found it in his heart to pity the creature as it stood there, stubborn, defiant, the blood pouring from its nostrils.

"Tire! Tire!" yelled Angus, who under stress had forgotten his English.

Asher succeeded in halting his excited horse. He raised his gun to his shoulder and sighted as he had been taught. The bull came charging towards them, but Asher and his horse held their ground. Then he fired. Again the animal received a hit in a vital spot. Instantly the shot was fired the horse stepped smartly out of the line of the buffalo's charge, nearly throwing its unprepared rider. But the buffalo too had stopped short, shaking its great shaggy head in a mournful and bewildered way. Then Angus, who had reloaded, gave the final shot, the *coup de grace,* and the big animal fell in a heap.

Angus pulled off the band that he had tied Indian fashion about his overlong hair and dropped it on the carcase so that they could claim it later.

"Suis-moi," he called to Asher and started off in the direction of a rise of ground. Here they reined in and watched the hunt.

Horsemen charged through the herd, their horses weaving among the madly stampeding bison. Once through the herd the horsemen wheeled around and charged through again over a field already strewn with dead and wounded buffalo.

Through the dust that was like the smoke of battle Asher watched one horseman make the run, loading with a flick of powder into the breech, a bullet spat from a mouthful down the muzzle, slammed home with a bang of the butt against the saddle, and the shot fired all in less time than it takes to tell it. He saw the horse swerve out of the way of the buffalo as it plunged forward and fell. Then rider and horse were off again, the hunter guiding his mount by the sway of his body while he reloaded his gun.

That's the way to ride and hunt, thought Asher, realizing that he and his horse were not always of one mind. He marvelled that this hunter brought a buffalo down with a single shot, whereas he and Angus had needed three to lay theirs low. Aloud he said:

"It is magnificent."

"Mais, oui," said Angus, "c'est certainement magnifique."

v

In less than an hour the buffalo run was over. The heads and legs of the kill were chopped off and left to the dogs and the wolves, while the women drove up with the carts to haul the carcases back to the camp. That night Asher feasted more successfully than the first time he had arrived in camp. The next day the women began cutting the meat into strips and preparing it for making pemmican, while the men loafed.

The two boys rode a little way out on the prairie and lay in the tall grass. Asher sitting up suddenly, watched Angus, utterly relaxed, staring at a cloud with eyes that had gone black and flattish like an Indian's.

"How could you even think of leaving all this to go to school?" he asked.

The familiar alert look returned to Angus's face and he rolled over, supporting himself on his elbows.

"I am told it is a good opportunity," he explained. "I have a patron in Montreal, a charitable person who has not seen me, but who has offered to pay for me at school."

He spoke in English, but he used words oddly—patron—charity. Probably in the eyes of the Metis Sam Mott had been his patron, thought Asher. Even now he was living on Sam's charity. He pushed the idea from him because it seemed complicated.

"Why are you called Angus?" he asked his friend. "That's a Scotch name."

Angus claimed a Scotch ancestor. But whether this Scottish agent of the Company had been his mother's father or grandfather, or whether he had taken an Indian or a Metis girl to wife Angus did not know. He only knew that this ancestor had existed and that he was called after him.

"We are the New Nation," he told Asher, "because we are made from all these other people. That is why we are called the Metis, the mixed people. If I go to school," continued Angus, "I will become a leader of the New Nation."

"Oh, nonsense," said Asher, "you don't need book learning to be a hunter."

"We hunt like Indians, but we think like white men. I might become a priest, or if I am not suited for a priest I might become a lawyer. The Hudson's Bay Company are our governors, but they respect such people."

"What you are saying is all politics," said Asher. "My father is a journalist and he writes about politics in his paper. He talks politics too, and lots of men come to his office and talk politics. But they are grown men, most of them quite old. Don't you think you're a little young for politics?"

"Don't you think you're a little young to be travelling alone in Rupert's Land with two horses and—"

Asher seized Angus half playfully round the waist and rolled over in the grass with him. He wanted to change the subject, also he wanted to find out which of them was the stronger.

They rolled, straining and struggling, each trying out the other's strength, each trying to keep on top. It was as Asher had suspected. The Metis boy had muscles of steel and he was quick. The slow anger began to rise in Asher, the feeling that sometimes gave him the extra strength and skill to finish a fight.

Suddenly Angus pushed him away and sprang to his feet.

"Why are we fighting?" he asked. "We are friends."

Asher looked at him in amazement. What kind of behaviour was this? The good fighting anger was surging up in him, but unless he came to grips again it would be wasted.

"I think you may be stronger than I am, but I want to find out."

"Asher," said Angus quickly, "there is something I must tell. Two wardens of the Hudson's Bay Company came to the camp today. First I think they only make a visit. But now I am sure—I know—they are after *you.*"

"What do you mean? What do they want with me?"

"They know maybe at Fort Garry that Mr. Mott is dead. They come to ask questions, maybe to take you away. If there is trouble, Asher, I am your friend." Angus held out his hand and Asher, beginning to feel uneasy, clasped it warmly.

"Our horses are here," said Angus. "I have pemmican in my saddle bags and we have our guns. If you like we will ride off to the Indians."

Asher looked across the rolling prairie and friendly bluffs beckoning them into the distance. He looked at their two horses and would have said yes but for an unpleasant thought. It was an idea that would not be shoved aside. It clapped a hand on his shoulder and looked him in the face.

"If I run off now they will say I am a thief. I will see these men and talk to them."

The business of the wardens proved far more complicated than Asher had expected. There was not only Sam

Mott's death, his property and his will, there was also the letter written by Josiah Mundy to the Hudson's Bay Company asking for the return of his son.

In the face of this warrant there was nothing his half-breed friends could do but wish him well. The wardens set out for Fort Garry taking with them Asher, the two horses, the Red River cart, all the baggage and the Cree-Metis, who had found Asher after Sam's death and was required as a witness.

Bitterly Asher regretted not having gone off with Angus to the Indians. This was what came of doing the right thing!

4. Fort Garry

I

PROMOTION IN the Hudson's Bay Company was slow and
as a result the factors of the Company's forts were men
of experience and proven ability. At the time the wardens brought Asher and his baggage into Fort Garry, the
chief factor was absent attending a meeting with the
Governor at Norway House. A subordinate was tem-
porarily in charge at Fort Garry.

This Thomas Dundurn had reason to feel that, even
allowing for Company policy, his promotion had been
exceptionally slow. It is sad to state that the manner
in which he dealt with the affair of Asher Mundy did
nothing to help him along. Indeed so unsatisfactory

did it prove that it brought the agent's career to a permanent standstill.

Thomas Dundurn had been brought up strictly and had spent his adult life under the half-military discipline of the Company. The idea of a boy running away from home was to his way of thinking almost criminal. When the boy in question had added to his bad conduct by taking a dead man's goods and going off to live with the half-breeds, Dundurn felt that this was just what one would expect.

Obviously the extraordinary affairs of Asher Mundy required investigation. An inquest was out of the question because there was no body, a trial because there was no judge or counsel. But Thomas Dundurn managed to combine a little of both in his proceedings.

He presided, Asher answered questions, the Cree-Metis was included as a witness, and since he spoke neither French nor English a missionary priest had been requested to act as an interpreter. A secretary recorded the evidence and a sixth person who had done business with Sam Mott was also present.

It quickly became apparent that Dundurn did not want explanations from the boy. He must answer yes or no.

"Is it true you ran away from home without your father's permission?"

"Yes, sir."

"Do you claim that the late Samuel Mott made you his heir?"

"Yes, sir."

"Have you a copy of his will?"

Asher attempted an explanation, brought out Sam's diary. But Dundurn slapped his hand on the table and insisted:

"Answer me directly. Have you his will?"

"No, sir."

"Do you know where it is?"

"No, sir."

"What was your relationship to the late Samuel Mott?"

Asher was briefly puzzled.

"He was my friend."

"Did he pay you wages?"

"No, sir. I was his apprentice. He paid my expenses."

"In short you were Samuel Mott's apprentice. You see you do not answer directly."

Dundurn then called on Mr. Trotter who had looked after Mott's business in Fort Garry. He asked him some questions about that and finally:

"Have you looked for a will among the effects of the late Mr. Mott stored in Fort Garry?"

"Yes, sir, I have."

"Did you find one?"

"I did not find one."

Dundurn then requested the priest to interpret for the Cree half-breed. By this means he learned how the Cree had found Asher with the body of Samuel Mott. Had the Cree seen the body? Yes. Did he recognize the man? Yes, he had seen him when he had come to the camp looking for the boy.

"Why was he looking for the boy in that camp?" asked Dundurn with an increase of interest.

The Cree's answer was not definite. He understood the boy had come to the camp because he was lost.

Would he say that while at the camp Mott and Asher were on good terms or on bad terms?

The priest translated this question and then entered into a little discussion with the Cree as though he was explaining something. Dundurn sharply requested him to give the Cree's reply directly.

"He says part of the time they seemed to be quarrelling."

Asher's head came up with a jerk.

"Now ask him," said Dundurn leaning forward, "if at the time he viewed the body of Samuel Mott he noticed any signs of violence on it?"

Asher sprang forward. "How dare you accuse me of murdering my friend!"

A gasp went round the room and Dundurn looked exceedingly annoyed.

"No accusation has been made," he said. "You, Asher Mundy, will be held here at Fort Garry until suitable arrangements can be made to return you to your father."

"I am not your prisoner," shouted Asher.

"Silence, Mundy. Your insolence will not be tolerated. You are not a prisoner, but you are in custody. A report of this evidence will be sent to the Governor of the Hudson's Bay Company and to the Attorney-General of Upper Canada."

Asher Mundy stood outside the chief factor's house feeling more completely unwanted than he had ever felt in his life. Dundurn's investigation had ended rather abruptly. No one had bothered to tell Asher what to do.

The French-Canadian priest, seeing him so forlorn, came over and spoke to him. He did not believe the boy was a liar and a thief, much less a murderer, and he had the curiosity common to people from the St. Lawrence valley in any kind of a legal tangle. Walking slowly back and forth before the factor's house they discussed Asher's problems.

"When did M'sieu Mott first speak to you of a will?"

"The day we were at Fort William. And it is so entered in his diary. But Mr. Dundurn has taken the diary away from me."

"There would be witnesses. Do you remember with whom he did business that day?"

Asher thought carefully. "There was Mr. McTavish, the factor, and he may have been with Mr. Masterman, the Governor's secretary."

"These men may know something. I will see what I can do."

"What do you think will be done with me, sir?" It was the first time Asher had ever talked with a priest and he was uncertain as to how to address him.

"Without doubt you will be sent home. Will you be glad to go home?"

"No, sir," said Asher soberly. "My father doesn't want me."

Somehow the pathetic little story did not go over so well this time.

"How can that be so?" said the priest mildly. "He makes himself great trouble to find you. You should write him a letter. That will travel faster out of this country than you will."

"Would that be permitted?"

"Write your letter. I will arrange the permission."

So Asher wrote a letter to his father.

My dear papa,
    I trust you are not angry with me for leaving home. I came out to Rupert's Land with Sam Mott to paint Indians, but Sam Mott died of inflammation of the lungs when we were alone on the prairie. That was a very hard blow. Sam made a will and made me his heir, but I cannot find the will. I was brought to Fort Garry by wardens and am held here by Mr. Dundurn who has some authority though he is not the factor. He will not listen to my explanations and treats me like a thief and thinks there was ill-will between me and Sam which of course there wasn't.
    I have formed a poor opinion of this gentleman which I think you would too if you were here. There is a Romish priest here who is my friend and thinks he can help me find the will. With resolution I hope to get out of these difficulties. I trust, dear papa, you are in good health and the others too. Give my kind regards to them and any of my friends,

Your respectful and obedient son,
ASHER MUNDY

Josiah Mundy received this letter in due course and also saw a copy of the report made by Thomas Dundurn. The letter he read with mixed feelings, but the report made him very angry. He began a series of articles in his newspaper criticizing the power and policies of the Hudson's Bay Company. This in turn greatly displeased Sir George Simpson, the Company's Governor. The Company ruled a vast territory, half a continent, which it kept entirely as a hunting ground. It did not want outsiders enquiring about this country. It did not want settlers. It did not want publicity, either good or bad. Mr. Mundy's articles were highly undesirable.

The Governor and Josiah Mundy agreed on only one point. Mr. Mundy wanted his son back and Sir George Simpson wanted the boy out of the country. But, as it turned out, this proved rather difficult even for the powerful Hudson's Bay Company. Because by this time Asher Mundy had run away again.

II

It came about in this way. Dundurn did not lock Asher up; jail accommodation was scarce in the North West. On the other hand he did not like to leave a slippery customer like Asher at large in Upper Fort Garry, where there was frequent traffic with St. Paul to the south in the territory of the United States.

He sent him twenty miles down river to the lower fort also known as the Stone Fort, the place where Asher and Sam Mott had first arrived in the country. Always careful for the interests of the Company, Dundurn saw no reason why Asher should not earn his keep. So he was put to work loading and unloading the York boats that supplied the forts of the interior via Lake Winnipeg and the Saskatchewan River.

"It is not interesting," said the shifty-eyed fellow working beside him, "after the fine free life on the prairie to find this!"

Asher pretended he did not understand French. He was sullen as a newly trapped animal and in no mood to be teased. But the man persisted, curious, but not unfriendly.

"Do they pay you wages?"

Asher shrugged.

"Is it true that you owned two horses?"

"Yes, and a Red River cart and a tent and a number of other things."

"And the Company took them all away from you."

"No matter. They are still mine."

"And will the Company pay you wages?"

"I don't know," said Asher indifferently. He nearly said that he had plenty of money (he had not been searched or had his personal baggage taken from him), but he did not trust this Joseph Labrie of the shifty eye.

Still you could not work beside a man without speaking, like a dumb ox. You could not eat and sleep with him and act as though he did not exist.

"Pemmican," said Joe Labrie, as they stowed away skin bags of that basic food of the North West. "A man could live a month on ten pounds and never be hungry."

"I have eaten pemmican," said Asher. "You exaggerate."

But Joe Labrie insisted on the wonderful qualities of pemmican and gave examples. All this had to be told slowly with repetitions and questions and answers back and forth. But Asher was really interested.

"No one will miss this," said Joe finally, rolling a stone-solid bag towards Asher with a piratical leer. "Take it and cache it."

So Asher took the skin-wrapped mould of pemmican and hid it in a corner of his bunk.

He asked Joe if it would be possible to find a group of hunters on the prairie.

"How large a band?" asked Joe.

"There would be several hundred—more than a hundred lodges," said Asher thinking of the Metis band he had left.

"No difficulty at all locating such a band once you struck the trail and if you had good mounts."

"But how would you find the trail?"

"Where did they start from? Fort Garry?"

"I don't know. I think not. I think it was Pembina."

"In that case," began Joe and launched into detail. Joe Labrie, Asher decided, knew the country.

Their discussion as usual was involved, requiring many questions and repetitions because of Asher's uncertain French. He thought a compass might be useful on such a journey. Sam had had one. But Joe considered a compass of no use, no doubt because he had never used one. At a point like this Joe Labrie was likely to break off abruptly as though he could not be expected to spend too much time talking to a mere boy.

Although Dundurn had said he was not a prisoner, Asher felt he was being treated like one. He spent a lot

of time planning escapes and imagining himself carrying them out. He spent his evenings checking over his
personal belongings, imagining a use for each item, keeping in readiness his fire-bag, his flints and tinder, powder
pouch and rifle balls—though he had no rifle. He made
these preparations merely to pass the time. He did
not seriously consider running away. He had no gun,
no horse, no tent, no friend.

"How would a man travel on the prairie without a
tent?"

"What need has a man for a tent?" asked Labrie. "He
rolls himself in his blanket and sleeps on evergreen or
willow boughs. There is usually something. Even in
winter men travel across the plains without tents."

"Now I know you are exaggerating," protested Asher.

"Not at all," said Labrie. "If you pass the winter in
this country you will see it yourself."

"What if it rains?" asked Asher, thinking of his own
dismal experience.

"Buffalo robe," answered Labrie. "Very good. Two
crotched sticks, a cross-bar and a few stones for anchor
and you have a small tent—if you are so delicate." He
demonstrated with large gestures.

On one of the unused bunks of their dormitory which
was intended to house more than the three or four men
who now used it, Asher found such a buffalo robe.

He shook it out, dislodging moths. They had done
some damage, but not too much. Asher spread the robe
out in the sun. No one took any notice of his activities.

"Do you plan to travel across the prairies this summer?" Asher at last asked desperately. Labrie's hints and silences were driving him frantic.

"No, no. Not at all. Don't have such ideas."

Asher felt as though a door had been slammed and bolted in his face. Shifty-eyed, untrustworthy, not even intelligent! Asher turned from Labrie in anger and contempt. Had he really been counting on Labrie? If he had his hope was gone. He could not travel on the prairie alone. He was secretly afraid of the country. But greater than his fear was the knowledge he would be pursued and brought back. That was a humiliation he could not face.

5. Two Horses

I

JOE LABRIE brought the saddle from the saddler and blacksmith shop where it had been repaired and dumped it by the ladder leading to their dormitory. He would, of course, take it presently to be locked up with the rest of the gear and harness belonging to the Company.

In a country where almost everyone at some time lived in the open and rarely had locks or bolts even for their houses, the Company was careful of its stores and goods. Everything was strictly accounted for and kept under lock. The livestock was stabled, although in the summer months Company horses were sometimes left all night outside the fort. Every night the great double

63

gates of the Stone Fort were barred, but in normal times no sentry kept guard.

Asher did not think anything of the saddle, although when he climbed up the ladder on his way to bed he was surprised to see it still lying there. He almost reminded Labrie that he had forgotten to lock it up.

Then he realized that this was the last piece in the escape puzzle. The game he had so often played in imagination could now be played in earnest, and this was the time.

There were a number of articles belonging to other people he was going to take tonight, including a horse. In the game, as he had played it in his mind, this was always excused by the fact that the Hudson's Bay Company in the first place had taken his possessions.

He now wrote a short letter pointing this out and asking the Company to make good any loss to itself or other persons. He signed this with his name and addressed it to the Chief Factor of Upper Fort Garry or To Whom It May Concern. The letter was written in a large sprawling hand by the feeble light that came through a window looking out on a clear starry night.

He could of course have paid for what he was taking with the bank notes in Sam's money belt. But he did not trust Joseph Labrie. He feared that if he left money neither it nor the letter would ever reach the chief factor.

Next he took Labrie's rifle which always stood by his bunk. Labrie was very proud of his gun and kept it well greased. Asher thought it a fine piece too as it was the same kind as his own and would carry the same size shot. He felt bad about taking the gun from Joe who had given him a lot of help even if he had failed him at the last step. On an impulse he took from his pocket Sam Mott's gold watch and left it in place of the gun. The watch must be quite valuable and Joe could get another rifle with it.

In his bunk Joe Labrie snored placidly and the two other men who shared the dormitory with them also slept soundly.

Asher made one pack of all his belongings, folding the blankets and buffalo robe round it. Through the rawhide thongs he used to bind it he slipped the gun. Then he fastened the whole with a tump-line and balanced it on his back as he had learned to do with the *voyageurs*.

Slowly and cautiously he climbed down the ladder, picking up the saddle as he left the building. Outside, the enclosure of the fort was quiet. The dogs, who knew him, stirred a little, but after a mild growl settled back to sleep.

His first hazard was the postern door in the big double gates. Was it locked or was it bolted? It proved to be bolted. He shot back the bolt and went through the door. He was out of the fort.

On a clear night in this open country it was not hard to find what he was looking for. Two horses were grazing close together. Asher approached one with gentle words. To his delight the animal seemed not only well fed and well cared for but docile too. It waited quietly till he came up, but then not liking a stranger cantered off. The other horse ran off too.

Asher unloosened his pack and left it with the saddle on the ground. Taking a length of rope he started after the horse. It waited till he was fairly close, then bolted off again. Asher whistled softly—used every word of cajolery and command he had heard among the plainsmen. Each time the horse waited, as though considering the matter, then bounded off.

From the horse's point of view it was likely all done in fun, but for Asher it was torture. Was he to spend the precious hours of the night chasing a horse? As his patience went, his movements became more and more awkward and futile. Finally the horse decided the game was over and allowed him to toss the lasso over its head and lead it—where? To the pack and saddle? But where had he left them? Why hadn't he thought to take his bearings when he laid them down? Now he would wander around in circles all night and be found by the first man awake at dawn. By one slip all his efforts would be brought to nothing.

Asher stood still, the leading rope looped over his arm. He looked at the fort, tried to reconstruct the path he had taken from the gate to where he had first seen the horses. If he had to wander around all night he would at least wander methodically.

By this means or by luck he found the pack and saddle and uttered a prayer of thanks. He saddled the horse clumsily but none the less successfully and bridled it with a bridle he had kept among his own things. The animal was restive, as though it considered these goings on in the dead of night unfair.

The other horse came back and looked on. Apparently these horses formed a pair. A strong desire rose in Asher to have them both. The Company had taken two horses from him. As he thought about this it became not only desirable but positively necessary to have two horses. If he was to outdistance possible pursuers he would need a fresh mount.

Oh, yes, but would the second horse want to play games too? Would he dare risk losing the saddled horse while he went after the other? The temptation to try was too great to resist. Taking the lasso he approached the second horse with beguiling words. The beast watched him without alarm and allowed him to drop the lasso over its head. Triumphantly he led it over to the saddled horse.

Then something he saw over at the fort caused him to turn cold even though he was hot and sweating from his exertions. A figure moved, outlined against the stone wall. By what freak of fortune could his escape have been discovered so soon? Had Joe Labrie only pretended to be asleep? Was he going to betray him?

He would not be taken back! Not at this point. Looping the reins and the rope over his arm so as to keep the horses near him, he reached for the rifle. Crazy idea! What use would it be except to rouse the whole fort. Besides, frantic as he was, he could hardly shoot Labrie with his own gun. He stood beside the two horses and

decided to fight for them with his bare hands if necessary. He would not be taken back! Not now.

While he stood waiting, desperation ebbed out of him
as he realized this moving creature was not human but
some animal—if indeed he had not imagined the whole
thing. Later he might laugh at himself, but he had gone
through too much anxiety and excitement this night to
feel anything but numb relief.

He must get away quickly. He had first thought of
fastening the pack on the back of the spare horse. But
this proved so difficult that he ended by tying it behind
the saddle of the horse he was to ride. He mounted,
looked for the north star, made some calculations with
the compass which he did not too clearly understand
and set off at an easy pace in what he was satisfied was
a south-westerly direction.

II

For the first time that night he experienced a feeling
of escape, a rapturous sense of freedom. The hated fort
disappeared in the distance. Overhead the starry firma-
ment wheeled slowly toward the dawn. First came the
grey light, then the gold. Asher rode with his back to
the sunrise and did not often look back to admire it.
He felt no sense of fatigue, but rather a wild exhilaration.
He was free, free.

He found the sprawling trail marks of what he believed to be the Metis band. At noon he halted by a lake
which seemed to have been their first night's camp. He
made a meal of berries and dry pemmican, watered his

horses and changed the saddle and pack to the second horse. Then he explored the site of the camp until he found the trail leading away from it and set out again.

Over-confidence was dangerous so he began to check over soberly all the steps he had taken. He wished he had left money instead of the gold watch for Labrie. The watch might prove an embarrassment to Joe. One slip, but not for him a dangerous one. In his fright last night he almost believed Joe had betrayed him. Now he wondered if Labrie had left the saddle out so as to help him escape. He had never known whether he could trust Joe or not and now he would never know. It was not likely he would ever see Joe Labrie again.

He hoped the horses belonged to the Company and not to someone who perhaps owned little else and who might have trouble extracting payment. The Company, which had Asher's possessions, never parted with anything without good reason. They were good horses. Oh yes, very good horses. Something about the saddle, now that he saw it in daylight—something familiar about a face glimpsed last evening at the officers' side of the fort flashed an appalling revelation into Asher's mind.

He had taken the wardens' horses!

That night he camped without fire, fearful of drawing attention. He hobbled the horses so that they would not wander away, spread his buffalo robe on the ground, rolled himself in his blankets and fell asleep, exhausted after riding a night and a day. Even so he woke several times to look about anxiously for the horses and to make sure his pack was safe. The country was full of wolves, the scavengers of the buffalo hunt, and he could hear them howling through the night far and near.

He continued on his way next morning, no longer free and joyful, but like a hunted fugitive with many a backward glance. The Hudson's Bay Company would never let him get away with its wardens' horses. He expected to see the wardens themselves freshly mounted riding over the prairie after him like avengers.

Still the horizon remained empty and the trail of the Metis hunters easy to follow.

From time to time Asher tried the rifle on wild fowl and rabbits, but not till the fourth day out did he bring down anything. It was a wild goose and whether he owed the hit to luck or increasing skill, he was very pleased. He would make a fire during the day when it could not be seen for any distance, pluck the bird and cut himself some choice pieces to roast on the end of a stick.

A prairie slough or lake lay in his path with a sandy beach at one end. Feeling more hopeful than he had for several days, Asher went swimming, lying afterwards on the sand to dry, listening to the lap of the water and the soft rustle of the bushes on the edge of the beach.

When the mosquitoes discovered him he dressed quickly and decided to ride farther before preparing the goose. He tied it to his saddle and mounted, riding up out of the hollow of the lake, through the rustling bushes that edged it and straight into a band of horsemen.

Wardens! thought Asher, horrified. But he was wrong. They were Indians.

He was relieved to see that they wore no war paint, but the way they closed in around him made him very uncomfortable. The parley promised to be long and complicated as he seemed to have less than a dozen words in common with them.

He tried to make them understand that he was on his way to the camp of the Metis hunters. The Indians, he believed, were Crees and so blood cousins of the Metis. He hoped to win their good will by letting them know that he too was in friendly association with the half-breeds.

Asher had no experience in dealing with Indians. He was uncomfortably aware that they sometimes kidnapped white boys and even children, keeping them hidden from their own people until they no longer wanted to leave the tribe. Fortunately they had not found him naked on the beach. He felt a certain confidence sitting astride his horse with the leading rope of the second animal securely looped around his wrist. Whatever happened nothing would induce him to dismount.

Now the Indians seemed to be talking about the Hudson's Bay Company. How let them know that the Company was no friend of his? But wait a minute. The Company was great and powerful and highly respected among the Indians. Wouldn't it be better to pretend to be a company agent?

Asher set about by word and gesture to persuade the Indians that he was travelling from Fort Garry to the Metis on Company business.

By nature and training acutely observant, the Indians were puzzled by him. He was too young to be a Company officer. He was too wild in his dress. But his language was English which was usual among the Company's servants, his horses were in good condition and the saddle was certainly a Company saddle. Besides, Asher conducted himself with an assurance and dignity that impressed them.

They were in no hurry to end the parley. He was likely the only human creature they would meet all day. They talked and pointed to the goose. What did they want with that? Then Asher realized that, as it was a particularly fine specimen, they wanted it for its feathers. They were willing to make a trade and offered him pemmican. But Asher refused it. He had plenty of pemmican, also he had heard that Indian pemmican was full of hairs and fur.

Then they produced a buffalo tongue rather unappetizingly wrapped in leaves that had become soaked through with blood. Asher looked it over and sniffed at it. It had been partially dried and seemed in fair condition. So he accepted it and the deal was closed. Two Indians insisted on accompanying him a little distance to make sure he was following the right trail. He was greatly relieved when they left him.

He made a fire while the sun was still high and roasted strips of the buffalo meat. Then he rode on through the long, long summer evening. The dusk came and the moon, first a pale white shadow, grew brighter and travelled up the sky.

He let the horses go more slowly, but still he rode on. He could not face another cheerless camp without fire, in fear of wolves, in fear of the wardens. The night was less terrifying if he kept moving. The idea took hold of him that if he did not find the Metis this night he would never find them. He had passed site after site where they had camped. He had seen the piles of bones and refuse from the buffalo hunts. Each time he had ridden all round the site, till he hit the main trail leading away from it. But he had not seen anywhere along the route the cairn of stones they had raised over Sam Mott's grave. Had he missed seeing it by chance or was he following a false trail? Was he hopelessly lost?

When he saw the half-breeds' camp in the distance he was afraid to believe it. It might be only a mirage of the moonlight. He rode towards it. There were the familiar shapes of the tepees and the circular wall of carts surrounding them. The dogs rushed out, barking, and the sleepy sentinels sprang alert from the camp fires, imagining a night attack. But it was only a boy with two horses.

When Asher came into the Ouellette lodge, Cyprian sat up among the buffalo robes and his wife also, wrapping a blanket around her. They took his return matter-of-factly. But there was welcome in Mama Ouellette's voice as she said sleepily: "Go and lie beside the other children." Cyprian reminded him: "Don't forget, Ashair, to unsaddle your horse." A practical man, Cyprian.

The family were all asleep when he returned to the tepee and rolled in beside the children. Angus was not

there, but questions would have to wait till morning.
Tired as he was, Asher deliberately kept himself awake
for a few minutes to feel the beautiful, the blessed sense
of homecoming.

III

Asher had hoped that once he found the hunters his
troubles would be over.   This hope was most happily
fulfilled.   All during the late golden summer and early
autumn he drifted across the prairie in a north-westerly
direction with the Ouellettes.   Sometimes they travelled alone, sometimes in the company of other hunters,
occasionally with a band of Crees.

Angus was no longer with his family. He had made his
decision and set out on the long journey to his school in
Lower Canada before Asher's return.   Asher missed his
friend, but not as much as he had expected.   One reason
may have been that he took Angus's place in the family.

Soon after he rejoined the hunters, the band began to
break up.   Many returned to Pembina. But the Ouellette
family were going farther west to a great western fort
called Edmonton and a mission called St. Albert, famous
among the Metis for its priest, Père Albert Lacombe.

There was a man to start things!   At St. Albert he had
built a church and a house and the Metis had built snug
houses for themselves.   There were tilled fields, better
than those of the Red River settlement.   At St. Albert
there was a bridge. Cyprian Ouellette had a great desire
to go there and see all this for himself.

This plan was most fortunate for Asher, for he too was headed determinedly west and this way he did not have to lose his family. They were a strange family for him to adopt, different in speech and race, primitive in their ways. But they were the people the self-willed boy had chosen.

Life with them was to his taste. No one interfered with him or told him what to do. No one found fault with him or laid down rules. There were no lessons and no chores. He learned the skills of a plainsman from Cyprian Ouellette, but without effort as though he absorbed them. He and Cyprian hunted for the family. Mama Ouellette, that wonderful woman, looked after everything else.

There was no need here for Sam Mott's watch. This life had its own time rhythms. As the summer slipped into autumn all greenness faded from the prairie and woodland; the country took on an endless variety of tawny browns and yellows. Wedge-shaped flights of wild geese passed overhead pointed south. Herds of buffalo moved in dust across the dry prairie seeking the wooded country along the rivers. Still Cyprian and his party held their course north-west.

Once a prairie fire raged orange red along the horizon. The Ouellette family fled before it towards the Saskatchewan, while all around them the wild life of the prairie fled with them. Mama Ouellette and the two older children rode the free horses. Cyprian and Asher drove the two unspeedy Red River carts piled with baggage and the two younger children, urging the unwilling ponies with whips and yells.

The prairie ended abruptly at a precipitous bank. Far below they saw the river flowing between surprisingly green poplar groves. Here they paused, hesitating to abandon the carts until the last minute. As they waited the wind shifted and the tide of fire swept elsewhere. After this scare they kept their course near the river.

Like the country the Metis also had changed colour. By the end of the summer they were sunburnt as dark as their Indian ancestors. Asher now understood the name they had given themselves and which they used oftener than any other, the *"bois-brulés,"* the "burnt-woods." Even the fair members of the Ouellette family were as dark as Mama herself, and Asher was as dark as any of them. He had grown even taller during the summer and had filled out. His father's buckskin shirt fitted him well now and was very shabby.

In an Indian tepee he saw a shirt of beautiful workmanship, soft as velvet, two wide strips of beading in intricate design down the front, two narrower strips in richest colours down the sleeves, fringed seams, a handsome shirt. When a giggling, round-faced Indian girl held it out to him, Asher instantly longed to own it. He engaged a fellow to interpret for him.

"Tell her," he said, "that I would like to buy the shirt."

The girl giggled more than ever and probably blushed. With an Indian it was hard to tell.

"She says it is not for sale."

"Then why is she showing it to me?"

"She says it is for her husband."

"Then will her husband sell it to me?"

"But she has no husband."

The girl's coyness began to raise dark suspicions in Asher's mind.

"What's wrong with her?" he asked his interpreter.

"How can I tell?" replied the man. "Women are foolish creatures, especially young ones. And this one is only a maid."

"Tell her," said Asher firmly, "that I am too young to marry, but I will buy the shirt."

But the girl only giggled and shook her head.

"Where is her mother? Perhaps she will sell it to me."

The mother when she came merely scolded the girl and was for packing her off shirt and all.

"What am I to do?" Asher asked his interpreter desperately. "I don't want the girl, but I want the shirt."

"What have you got to show them? You have not offered anything yet."

Asher raced to his baggage and returned with a shiny gold coin set in its metal loop and furnished with a cord —a necklace. After a little he brought out its mate. Now they were earrings to hang dangling from a lady's ear.

The girl reached her hand out eagerly, her longing for adornment burning as high as Asher's, her husband hunger forgotten. The exchange was made. Asher lovingly folded the shirt and placed it among his things to be worn only on the greatest occasions.

The last flights of geese had passed overhead. After weeks filled with their honking cry the monotonous creak-screech of the carts made itself heard again. It had become a homey sound to Asher, although it had once set his teeth on edge. The nights were setting in early and the mornings were cool, but the middle of the day was still hot and golden like the centre of a fire that is beginning to die around the edges, when Asher and the Ouellette family arrived at Fort Edmonton.

6. Fort Edmonton

HERE AT LAST was a place where there was something to see, where something was always happening, new people arriving, the brigade expected. Cyprian Ouellette went out to visit St. Albert and saw the bridge and the church. In the spring perhaps he might move there, when he could build a house during the summer. But certainly Fort Edmonton was the place to pass the winter. Frankly he considered it as fine as Fort Garry. True it did not have stone walls, but the chief factor's house for size and furnishing was without equal anywhere in the North West. Imagine finding such a place so far from the Red River country!

Asher, who did not have a high opinion of Fort Garry either Upper or Lower, did not express an opinion on Fort Edmonton. He hoped to do better than pass the winter there.

The last brigade of the season came up the Saskatchewan bringing the chief factor. This was a brigade of York boats, such as Asher had helped to load and unload at Fort Garry. A crew of eight men working in shifts, rowed, poled, towed or tracked these boats along the rivers of Rupert's Land. Occasionally on the lakes they sailed them. But for the most part working on the York boats was the greatest drudgery the *voyageurs* were called on to do.

Nevertheless their high spirits overcame even slavish work. True to their traditions, when they came to a fort they tried whenever possible to make a picturesque entrance, donning their red woollen shirts and bright sashes, roaring out their French songs.

The people of Fort Edmonton heard the *voyageurs'* songs even before they saw them, poling their boats round the bend of the river. The fort was in a state of high excitement. The Company's flag, with the Union Jack in one corner and the initials H. B. C. in the other, flew in the breeze. The cannon in the bastions were primed for the salute of honour. The chief factor's Indian wife and his children were at the landing to meet him as well as the steward of the fort and the clerks. His boat was brought to the landing first. After distributing embraces and handshakes suitably he proceeded up the hill to the fort, surrounded by his family and the Company's employees. The little cannon boomed their salute, while the *voyageurs* swarmed up from the landing place, boastful and gay, all set for a celebration.

This was, Asher was willing to agree, a sight worth seeing. He paid special attention to Chief Factor Rowand, who, unlike the Governor and the factors of the Red River country with their cloth coats and top hats, dressed in the style of the North West, moccasins, buckskin shirt and a brimless deerskin cap. He was a ruddy-faced, stoutish man, who on this occasion was in a genial good humour. Asher decided he would avoid this man and leave Fort Edmonton on the first opportunity.

He imagined that during the summer he had acquired an impenetrable disguise. The boy who had come into Rupert's Land in early summer had disappeared. In his place was a *bois-brulé*, long-haired, dressed in buckskins. Even his name had gone. He now preferred to call himself Deuxchevaux, in boastful reference to his ownership of two horses. The name appealed to the imagination and humour of the Metis and they readily accepted it. He felt that for the present at least there was no danger of discovery.

He underestimated the Hudson's Bay Company. All the factors including Chief Factor Rowand had received instructions and information regarding the boy Asher Mundy, as well as the tip that he might be travelling with a half-breed family called Ouellette. When Mr. Rowand saw the name of Cyprian Ouellette listed as a family man employed at the fort as a builder, he immediately asked:

"Has the Ouellette family been at Fort Edmonton long?"

"No, sir," replied the clerk. "Only about a fortnight."

"Have they an English boy with them about fifteen or sixteen years of age?"

"They have a boy about that age with them. He goes by the name of Deuxchevaux. Now that you mention it, Mr. Rowand, I think that boy understands English quite well."

"Thank you, Mr. Stewart. Will you kindly have Mr. Two Horses sent to me directly. We'll see if he understands me."

Brought into the Chief Factor's office, Asher found himself under the scrutiny of a pair of piercing blue eyes. He, on his part, tried to take the measure of this new officer of the Company who had caught up with him. Mr. Rowand, he decided, in spite of his genial expression was not a man to fool with.

"Are you Asher Mundy?"

"Yes, sir."

"Sit down."

At least this man wasn't a second Dundurn.

"I have news for you. Mr. Mott's will has been found and your claim to be his heir is sustained."

Asher could not help smiling with pleasure.

"That is good news, indeed, sir."

"You would have learnt it sooner if you had stayed at Fort Garry. Are you aware you took the wardens' horses?"

"I—I realized that afterwards. You must understand, sir, the Company had taken my horses first."

"Mmm-m. Had ye ever thought of being a trader?"

"No, sir."

"Just as well perhaps. Your methods wouldn't suit the Company. As you ought to know, your father wants you back. Why does he want you?"

"I'm sure I don't know."

"I don't either. You're too old to keep at home. He'll only have to launch you out again. However, he has a right to some say in the matter. I have definite instructions regarding you. Until you can be sent out of the country, you are to be considered a ward of the Company and to be treated as a gentleman. A gentleman, mind you." The Chief Factor looked at the unkempt *bois-brulé* and there was no doubt about the twinkle in the frosty blue eye. "So you will gather up your things, wherever they are, and take them over to Bachelors' Hall. Find Mr. Rush. He will assign you quarters. And now, young Mundy, I have one order for you which must be followed strictly. Under no circumstances may you leave the fort except by my permission. Is that clear?"

"Yes, sir."

II

Three days later a company of horsemen and pack horses left Fort Edmonton before dawn, setting out for Rocky Mountain House, the last Company fort east of the mountains. A few miles from the fort they were joined by travellers from St. Albert, Father Lacombe on a mission to the Blackfoot Indians, Alexis his guide, and several Metis who hoped to find jobs with a late brigade going through the mountains before the winter set in.

Somewhere near the point where the party from St. Albert joined the party from the fort, Asher Mundy added himself to the number. He had not deliberately planned an escape any more than he had planned his escape from Fort Garry. But when a good chance to get away had turned up he had taken it.

No one paid much attention to him. The people from the fort thought he had come from St. Albert. Those from St. Albert assumed that he belonged to the party from the fort. He made himself useful in various small ways; he was quite good at this kind of thing when he chose. And he did not talk much. He did not really expect to succeed, but after three days had passed and he was casually accepted by everyone he could not help congratulating himself on his bold and resolute course.

Great bare hills, enormous hills rose on all sides of them. These were not the mountains, but the foothills of the mountains, the country of the Blackfoot Indians, the splendid warriors and horsemen whom Sam Mott had planned to visit. So far none of them had appeared, but Asher understood that they often visited Rocky Mountain House.

As they rode through the hills the thin bracing air of these altitudes ran through his blood like wine. He felt he could ride like this forever; nothing seemed impossible. The most grandiose schemes filled his mind. He would attach himself to a brigade going through the mountains, work as a *voyageur,* visit the places and tribes of the Pacific coast as Sam had planned.

One day as they reached the crest of a high hill he saw along the edge of the distant horizon white triangles, like a row of jagged teeth. As he stared at this sight, wondering, the men before him in the line of march spread out, preparing to halt for a meal.

"Are those the Rocky Mountains?" Asher asked in a low voice of a man next to him.

"That's them."

Asher could not keep from asking more questions.

"Is it true that on the other side of the mountains it is always summer?"

The man said he had seen roses blooming at Fort Vancouver on Christmas day. It was a green and pleasant country where life was easy.

But his neighbour said it was a vile climate, mist and rain and darkness, forests of unbelievable denseness all around. A man lived smothered in gloom. A great argument arose. Obviously Asher would have to go to this country himself to find out the truth about it.

One evening they asked Father Lacombe to tell them a story. He was famous as a story-teller and had had many extraordinary experiences among the Indians. If the story he told them was not the kind they expected it nevertheless held their interest to the end.

"A certain Indian girl," he began, "formed a union with a white man, a marriage, as they say, after the custom of the country. After a time he left her and went away. She returned to her tribe taking her child with her. This child was brought up in the tribe though everyone knew he had a white father and the boy knew it also. Then one day when he was almost grown to manhood the mother said: 'There are white men camping nearby and one of them is your father.' She told him his name. We shall call him Blanc.

"The young man was delighted as he had always wanted to know his father. So he put on his finest shirt and moccasins and made himself as handsome as possible. He set out in the evening when the white men would be in camp. When he arrived there he was uneasy as he was more accustomed to Indian ways than white ways. But he asked for Mr. Blanc and when he was questioned as to his business said his mother had told him Mr. Blanc was his father.

"The man who took this message went into the tent and left him standing outside. Presently the young man heard the white men laughing and talking in their own language which he understood only a little.

" 'There's a young half-breed out there,' one was saying. 'All dressed up. He is asking to see you. He says he's your son.'

"Mr. Blanc came out and talked to the young man for a few minutes. Then he went back into the tent. And again the young man was not invited in.

" 'Well, what do you think of your son?' the other asked Blanc. 'Don't you think he looks like you?'

" 'He may well be my son,' said Blanc.

" 'Then aren't you going to do something for him? At least give him something?'

" 'No,' said Mr. Blanc. 'Why should I? Too many years have passed to prove anything. If I give him anything he may follow me for more. If I do not he will go away.'

"He then made some joke and again there was laughter inside the tent.

"The young man waited outside a while, but when his father did not come out to speak to him or invite him in, he went away sadly. Nor did he ever try to see his father again or any longer take pride in his white blood."

When the story was ended the men remained silent realizing that Father Lacombe had played a little trick on them and given them a sermon instead of a story. Also they were thoughtful for some of them had made unions with Indian women such as described and had deserted them and their children.

Asher thought it was as sad a story as he had ever heard. He could not imagine such hard-heartedness. His own father, no matter how much fault he might find with him, would never reject him. Nor would Cyprian behave so to Angus. But that Scotch ancestor of Angus's, that grandfather that Angus didn't know much about except his name, perhaps he had been such a man.

Then Asher's thoughts turned uneasily to himself. He sometimes feared he was behaving rather badly towards his own father. Oh, well, when he reached the Pacific coast he would write his father another letter giving an account of all his adventures. The thought of these adventures, the ones he had had and the ones he expected to have soon cheered him up.

But alas for his plans, luck turned against him. They were less than a day's journey from Rocky Mountain House when two horsemen galloped up and claimed the runaway in the name of Chief Factor Rowand. Fort Edmonton, unlike Fort Garry, did not have wardens, so Mr. Rowand had sent two of his clerks.

It was a humiliating moment for Asher before all these men with whom he had been ingratiating himself. It was a bitter disappointment after a glimpse of the Rockies to have to turn back. Deep in his heart he vowed that some day, somehow, he would travel through those mountains. The return journey did not take long. It was all downhill. Oh, the humiliation of the whole business!

Under the circumstances Chief Factor Rowand was not a pleasant person to face. He was in a towering rage. This time he did not ask Asher to sit down. He left him standing so that he might feel the affect of several seconds of silent anger.

"You were given fair and honourable treatment here," began Rowand. "And you abused it. If I chose it would be quite proper to treat you as a prisoner and with the greatest severity. I will exact from you a formal promise not to run away again. Is it possible that you do not understand these things? Shall I explain to you exactly what is meant by a promise—your word of honour—a parole?"

"No, sir," replied Asher haughtily. "I understand what you mean, but I am not giving you my promise."

At these words, Mr. Rowand's face, naturally ruddy, turned purple. It was an alarming thing to see. Asher feared that the man was going to fall into some kind of fit.

"You will have half an hour to make up your mind," he said at last. "Half an hour by the clock in the great hall. If you are not a fool you'll accept the terms any honourable man would be willing to accept. If not —I do not argue with the people under my charge. I do not argue with boys. If you give me trouble, Asher Mundy, by God, I'll have you flogged!"

Mr. Rowand left Asher alone to think about this and walked out onto the gallery surrounding the second floor of the house. He felt the need to cool off. The sight of his well-built house, of the Bachelors' Hall to the right and the Indian Hall to the left, the sturdy stockade with its bastions and cannon, the sight of the people of the fort going about their affairs, had a calming effect. Everywhere he looked an orderly disciplined little world met his glance.

He had been furious to find himself defied by a fifteen-year-old boy. Should the lad persist in his defiance it would not only be infuriating, it would be awkward. There was no jail where he could lock him up nor anyone to whom he could give the tiresome task of guarding him. Besides, his instructions had been to treat the boy kindly.

His concern proved needless. In the clash of wills between the man and the boy the man's will proved the stronger. Asher gave him the promise. To impress on him its importance Rowand had him make it in the presence of two witnesses. Then as often happens with men of quick fierce temper, Rowand's good humour returned and he became the genial person Asher had first seen coming up from the boats.

"I have something to show you," he said. He took Asher to the gentlemen's mess hall, a large splendid room with an enormous fireplace and auxiliary stoves for winter heating. It was sparsely furnished with the necessary chairs, table and sideboard, but lavishly decorated. The ceiling was painted in bold highly coloured designs, guns and hunting trophies were arranged over the fireplace and several large paintings hung on the walls. When Asher saw these paintings he had eyes for nothing else.

"This is what I thought you would like to see," said the Chief Factor. "Samuel Mott's paintings of the Black-foot Indians."

"Was Sam Mott ever at Fort Edmonton?"

"Yes, indeed. About fifteen years ago. He did these at the fort. Didn't you travel with him in some capacity?"

"I was his pupil."

"Then you paint and draw too?"

"All my drawing materials were left at Fort Garry," replied Asher shortly.

Rowand made some other remarks about the hall and the guests who had been entertained there. Then he left Asher walking up and down the room, looking at the pictures. A strange boy. Probably hadn't heard a word he had said.

Asher continued to stare at the pictures. First the missionary and his story of the father, now the Chief Factor showing him Sam Mott's paintings. Running away was proving more complicated than he had expected.

III

They came along the south bank of the river, a cavalcade of Blackfoot Indians, their sure-footed horses feeling their way down the narrow path, their metal ornaments flashing in the sun, their blankets and feathers gay as a circus. They forded the Saskatchewan and came up the path to the fort at the same deliberate pace, sitting their horses with insolent ease. "They are the best-looking, the best mounted, the best accoutred, the most warlike of all the tribes I have encountered," Sam Mott had said of them.

The Blackfeet were showmen. Upon the meadow before the fort the young bloods careened about. Even in a country of horsemen their horsemanship was notable. In the rear the older women with the children and the heavy baggage got themselves across the river on rafts. While the business of pitching camp was briskly carried out, the chiefs in full ceremonial costume came into the fort and were received by the Chief Factor in the gentlemen's mess hall.

Asher hung about the gallery watching through one of the windows. It was an undignified thing for him to do, but the scene inside fascinated him. He studied the proud, strong-nosed faces of the chiefs and compared them with the paintings on the walls. He took in the details of their beaded tunics and feathered head dress and considered how he would have treated them if he had been privileged to work on Sam Mott's canvases.

If Sam had lived they would have been invited into the mess hall to meet the chiefs. The handsome costumes would have been put on and the fine attitudes struck for them. The Indians would have watched with respect while Sam made his sketches, practised his medicine. Regret like physical pain bit into Asher. Why had not Sam lived to reach what he had come so far to find? Why had things gone wrong for them both?

In the hall Chief Factor Rowand exchanged elaborate greetings, ceremoniously smoked the pipe of peace, listened through his interpreter to a great deal of what Asher would have called politics, and made answer. He fervently wished the Blackfeet had not come. It was the wrong season; they had few furs to trade. Fort Edmonton was not Blackfoot territory like Rocky Mountain House. The country around Fort Edmonton was full of possible enemies, Crees and Assiniboines. Rowand did not want an Indian war on his doorstep.

Already the Blackfoot chiefs were complaining that the white traders favoured their enemies, sheltered the Crees within their fort and received the Blackfeet like strangers. Rowand assured them civilly that they were welcome.

The Indian Hall was opened for the trading. Goods were placed on the shelves, but not too much, as the Chief Factor did not want the Indians to linger. Tobacco was provided and rum, carefully diluted with water as was the practice of the Company. Orders were sent to a small band of Crees cutting wood about a mile away not to come to the fort while the Blackfeet were there. The horses were crowded into a stockade inside the walls; the Blackfeet considered horse stealing honourable sport.

But these precautions could not provide for every possibility. Three mounted Crees, probably seeking vengeance for the death of a relative, whipped round the corner of the fort and fired on a Blackfoot man and woman, among the last to leave the fort, then fled unpursued. The man dropped in the dust, seriously wounded, and was carried into the fort, followed by his wailing squaw.

Chief Factor Rowand sent for the chiefs and asked them if they wished the man to be treated at the fort or returned to the camp. When the Blackfeet chose to have the man carried away, he dared not even send remedies for fear that, if the Indian died, it would be blamed on white medicine. But the woman he loaded with gifts.

Another day passed and still the Blackfoot camp remained. The Chief Factor seeing it from the gallery of his house found it an offence to his eye. Not so Asher. He decided to visit the camp.

While the trading had been going on he had been kept busy running messages from one part of the fort to another for Rowand. As he was quick and intelligent the work had given satisfaction to both of them.

He had no reason to complain of his treatment at Fort Edmonton. Apart from the promise that had been exacted of him not to run away, he had been left as free as even he could wish. He had a bed at Bachelors' Hall and took his meals at the gentlemen's mess whenever he wished. But when he tired of the company of the young Scottish clerks he could always return to the amiable Ouellette family.

He was free to come and go in and about the fort. Rowand sometimes took him hunting. He had been to St. Albert with Cyprian. There seemed no reason why he should not visit the Blackfoot camp. He took Sam's compass with him on the chance of trading and, as was proper under the circumstances, he went unarmed.

A strange feeling of having crossed an invisible boundary came over him as he approached the camp. Perhaps he should not have come alone. But he was too proud to turn back. As he came to the first tepees the half-wild dogs rushed out at him. He drove them off boldly. He was not afraid of Indian dogs. This place was not like the lounging, easy-going Indian camps he was used to. No one was about. Then round a tepee came five or six young braves, some not much older than Asher. He was stunned to see their faces streaked with vermilion war paint. What could have happened?

They came at him, jeering and hooting. Without swerving from his path Asher continued on his way, head high, determined to ignore them. One of the young Blackfeet stuck out his foot, attempting to trip him. Asher recovered himself before he sprawled on his face and backed away from them, doubling up his fists.

What should he do? Try to knock out several in the hope that some older and more sensible person would come to his rescue? The Blackfeet were on a peaceable trading visit. This must be a crude joke.

Backing as close as he could to a tepee, Asher faced his tormentors. Still hooting they hung back a little, then closed in on him. He knocked down one with a successful upper-cut to the jaw, sent another reeling backward with a well-aimed kick, saw on his right the flash of a tomahawk and turned in time to seize the raised arm. This was not going to be a fair fight nor was it going to last long. An arm shot out behind him and instead of the shattering blow his quivering nerves expected he found himself yanked into the dark interior of the tepee. A voice, reassuringly French, exclaimed:

"*Sacré bleu!* Is the boy trying to get himself killed!"

Two hands seized his shoulders and swung him around. "Ashair!" continued the voice, surprised. Asher had just time to cry "Napoleon!" in joyful recognition when he was swept into an embrace smelling comfortably of grease and tobacco. He emerged, gasping:

"Napoleon Boucher, what are you doing here?"

"Ah-ha! What are *you* doing here? It doesn't matter.
We are both going to leave fast. Sa mère," the *voyageur* called to the old woman who stood at the entrance,
having ordered away the young braves, "get us out of
here."

There were other occupants in the tent, but the light
was poor and afterwards Asher only remembered the
old woman. She gave them each a blanket to wrap themselves in. She made them stay quiet for a while; then,
after she was sure no one was lingering about outside,
she drew her own blanket over her head and led them
out. She dodged here and there among the tepees,
Napoleon and Asher following her, wrapped in their
blankets, trying to look like two squaws, with what success may be imagined. When they came to the edge of
the camp nearest the fort the old woman thriftily took
the blankets and left them.

"No false pride now," said Napoleon. "We run for it."

Run they did at a sprinter's pace toward the fort. Not
until they were within safe distance of the gate did they
slow down.

"Not very dignified, that!" grumbled Napoleon. "If it
had not been for you I would have walked out boldly.
They understand the bold manner. But things are bad
in that camp, eh? Something has gone wrong."

"Perhaps the man who was wounded died. How glad
I am to see you, Napoleon! When did you get here?"

"Only yesterday. I came with a brigade to Fort Pitt—
tracking—with York boats. What travail! You cannot
imagine it. Then I came on here, but by an easier way,

I assure you. No more tracking for Napoleon Boucher. I'm glad to see you again, Ashair," he continued, throwing an arm affectionately about Asher's shoulders. "And what of M'sieu Mott?"

"Oh, Napoleon, didn't you hear? He died of a fever when we were crossing the prairie early in the summer."

"I had heard something of that, but I had hoped it was not true. We have much to tell each other, but it must wait. It is necessary to make a report to M. le Facteur about what is going on among those savages."

"Oblige me, Nap. Don't say anything about my being there."

It suddenly occurred to Asher that Rowand had forbidden anyone to visit the Blackfoot camp. Until this minute he had quite forgotten the order. Knowing the Chief Factor's temper he doubted that he would be able to make him understand that.

IV

Chief Factor Rowand was too busy with more important matters to bother about the misdemeanours of his junior aide. A large war party of Blackfeet, gathering strength as it went—the latest report estimated seven hundred warriors—was riding up from the southern country headed for Fort Edmonton.

Some time during the past week a little party of Blackfeet, who had unwisely separated from the trading band, had been literally cut to pieces not many miles from the fort and their hands and feet hung ghoulishly from nearby bushes.

Who had committed the outrage? None of the local tribes had an alliance with the Blackfeet at that time. Suspicion fell on the Assiniboines. But according to Blackfoot thinking the fort was the proper object of vengeance. It encouraged the presence of other tribes and sheltered them. Also the fort stayed put; a war party could easily find it. The Blackfeet did not hesitate to attack a fort when they were in force. They had a dangerous record of success in this kind of warfare.

Even while the Chief Factor was listening to Napoleon Boucher's story and issuing instructions for the defence, one of the clerks reported that the Cree woodcutters with their families were at the gate expecting admission.

"Certainly admit them," said Rowand. "We can't leave them to be massacred by the war party when it arrives. Also I don't want them attacking the Blackfoot camp. We may still settle this peaceably."

To this end he sent off a messenger to Father Lacombe, who knew the Blackfoot language and had won their respect.

Asher got his rifle and followed Napoleon to the stockade.

"As a man of courage," said Napoleon, "I shall choose a place of great danger."

"That's all right," answered Asher. "I'm not afraid." Napoleon did not need to be so boastful.

They climbed the ladder leading to the bastion looking toward the Blackfoot camp and stationed themselves at the rifle slots.

"What do you think is likely to happen, Nap?"

"Nothing till dark. They may attack with fire arrows. They'll creep as close as they can, then they'll rush the gates."

"They couldn't overcome us, could they?"

"Oh, never," said Napoleon with conviction.

It had been a cold grey day and the evening set in early.

"It may snow," said Asher.

"It is possible."

"Will that stop them?"

"Not at all."

It was growing darker. On the south side of the river the camp fires of the war party began to glow far along the bank. Three more men joined them in the bastion. they talked, but not much. How patient they were. How quietly they stood by the rifle slots watching, watching and listening.

Asher had not imagined war would be like this. In the many stories of battle he had read, the people concerned had dashed against each other to great purpose. The trouble was that Asher found it hard to keep still. He fidgeted and wiggled. He thought of Cyprian standing somewhere along the wall with his rifle, quiet and steady. He wondered if it would have been more comradely of him to have sought out his good friend of the summer to fight by his side. Of course he hadn't thought. He had simply as a matter of course followed the gaudy Napoleon into the bastion.

This damned waiting! When would it be over? Then he remembered what they were waiting for. He was not afraid, but on the other hand he didn't feel particularly brave. It was getting colder. He tried to be like the alert, quiet men around him. But this only made the fidgets worse.

The Chief Factor on a quick tour of the defences passed along the platform below the bastion.

"Mundy," he called. "Come down out of there. I need you for my courier."

"Yes, sir," said Asher, quickly scrambling down the ladder. At that moment he positively liked Mr. Rowand.

Now that he was attached to general staff, so to speak, he was kept mercifully active. The fort was full to bursting with people. Rowand had the women carrying buckets of water to strategic points in case of a fire attack.

Horsemen pounded up to the gate farthest from the river and the Blackfoot camp. They were Père Lacombe and twenty armed Metis from St. Albert.

"Thank God you were not ambushed," said Rowand when he greeted them. "I was afraid they had already surrounded us. The war party is in force across the river. They must not yet have crossed over."

"Ah, my poor Blackfeet," said the priest. "What madness! Did you know we met three survivors of the massacre, my Alexis and I, three miserable creatures, wounded, without food or weapons? We dressed their wounds and lent them our horses. We are partly responsible for this, for apparently when the poor creatures reached their people their story roused them to vengeance. I will speak to them."

"Indeed, Father, I had hoped we could summon them to a conference, but the darkness came too quickly. Anyone who stepped out of the south gate of the fort would be killed."

"But you must stay here—naturally. You are responsible for the fort. I will go out and speak to them. They know my voice and I shall speak very loudly."

"It is a generous offer, but impossible. I cannot consent to useless sacrifice. We are well armed and fully on guard. We can sustain the attack of a thousand Blackfeet—if there should be that many of them."

"I am not a soldier, M'sieu Rowand. Fort Bow sustained the first attack, but not the following ones. Is that not so?"

"That was different," said Rowand quickly. "Fort Bow was afire."

"And will not this fort be afire too? M'sieu Rowand, when that time comes the defenders will fight with reckless courage. You will. This boy beside you will. But I am not a fighting man. I must perform my reckless act now. Please God it will help."

Without waiting for formal consent Père Lacombe left them and walked with firm quick step towards the south gate. Such was his prestige among all the people of the high prairie country that he had his way. The gate was unbarred and opened a crack at his word. He passed through and it was closed after him.

There goes a brave man, thought Asher. I would not like to go out into that darkness.

"Take a message, Mundy," said the Chief Factor, "to the men along the south wall to listen for the priest's voice and hold their fire."

Asher Mundy ran along the platform that extended round the inside of the stockade about half-way from the top. Before he had completed his errand a spatter of bullets hit the outside wall. Then a thrill went through him as a voice began to call on the meadow before the fort. Clear and vibrant came the short, harsh-sounding phrases in Blackfoot, a language incomprehensible to almost everyone in the fort where Cree was the familiar Indian dialect.

"I am he you call Arsous-kitsi-rarpi, the man of good heart. Hear me, I am Arsous-kitsi-rarpi.

"I came into your tents when the plague was there. I nursed your sick. Ask those I helped. They are with you.

"I am Arsous-kitsi-rarpi. I gave my horse and food to your kinsmen last week. I bound their wounds. Ask them. They are with you.

"I am Arsous-kitsi-rarpi. You must not attack the white man's fort. They are my brothers. They do not shelter the murderers of your kin. They will punish them.

"I am Arsous-kitsi-rarpi. Hear me. Send your chiefs to meet the white chief to speak words of peace.

"I am Arsous-kitsi-rarpi. Hear me. These men are my brothers—"

For two hours the strange phrases sounded up and down the meadow before the fort. Then Father Lacombe, hoarse and exhausted, returned. He had not been shot at after the first outburst, but no Blackfoot chief had accepted his invitation to make peace.

"Perhaps they wait for daylight," said the priest.

All night men stood to their posts along the walls. The hours passed. Sometimes the Indians chose to attack just before dawn. Looking up into the cloudy night sky one after another of the defenders fancied it was a little paler, a little greyer. Then there could be no doubt about it. Morning was here.

As the meadows, the river valley, the horizon became visible the defenders saw that the Indian encampment on the fort side was gone. Across the river thin wisps of smoke rose from deserted camp fires. The Blackfeet were gone. The Chief Factor looking through a spy glass from the gallery of his house saw only trampled grass and churned up earth on the spot where the sight of the Indian camp had offended his eyes for days. The Blackfeet had disappeared into the vast prairies. Before nightfall the snow came, thin, driving snow.

v

It was Christmas Eve and practically everyone in Fort Edmonton was at midnight mass, from the Chief Factor and his family in the front seats to Asher Mundy in the rear with several youths who like him were not sure they could last out the service. He was wearing new moccasins, new buffalo-skin leggings, the hand-made gift of Mama Ouellette, and he had on his magnificent Indian shirt. He had distributed the wooden toys he had carved and painted himself to the younger Ouellette children and to the Rowand children. To Mama Ouellette he had given a pair of gold coins set as earrings.

The children's choir trained by Father Lacombe repaid his enthusiasm with a hearty if uneven singing of the responses and old French carols. As he turned from time to time to include the congregation in the mass, the missionary beamed on them all. This is what he loved above all things, to be celebrating mass on a great feast surrounded by his flock.

Asher stood at the back of the chapel in his holiday clothes looking sullen and feeling lonely, although he didn't know what was the matter with him. He had come a thousand miles from home and was as discontented now as he had been then. He thought of his family, his brother and sisters and how they would spend Christmas. Would they miss him and speak of him, the lost one? Was his father angry with him? He thought of Sam Mott and how he had wanted Asher to go away to Europe and be taught the artist's craft as he had learned it. He wondered if Sam would be angry with him because he had not followed his advice. He had been a bad son and a false friend.

Depression settled over him. This was what happened when he got stuck some place where he had nothing to do but think. Asher Mundy had no use for thinking. He considered leaving the church but he had nowhere to go. It is true that the Scottish clerks were having a little party by themselves, but Asher knew that young men of nineteen and twenty did not welcome boys of

fifteen into their exclusive company. He stayed and
suffered his thoughts.

After mass the congregation lingered outside. Those
who had come from St. Albert were waiting to carry
Father Lacombe back for the mass at dawn. The
people of Fort Edmonton were exchanging greetings
and the Chief Factor and his wife moved among them.
It was only on important occasions like this that they
appeared together. Indian and Metis women usually
remained in the background. But Mrs. Rowand was the
daughter of a Cree chief and the wife of a Chief Factor,
married not merely "according to the custom of the
country" but with the full rites of the Church and all the
authority of the white man's laws. On occasions like this
she bore herself with dignity, aware of her position.

"Merry Christmas, Mundy," she said, seeing the boy
in the crowd.

"Merry Christmas," called the Chief Factor. "Don't
look so glum, boy. You'll be coming to the Christmas dinner, of course."

"Oh, thank you, Mr. Rowand," said Asher, who for
some days had been wondering how he could get himself included in the Chief Factor's festivities. "Merry
Christmas, sir. And Merry Christmas to you, ma'am."

Suddenly he felt more cheerful. Suddenly it *was* a
Merry Christmas; he began exchanging greetings all
around.

It was at the Chief Factor's Christmas party that Asher
Mundy decided to become an Arctic explorer.

John Rowand, dressed in a suit with coat of fine green cloth and a ruffled linen shirt immaculately laundered, received his guests, those who, according to the standards of the Hudson's Bay Company, were the gentlemen of the district. They were not a numerous company, the steward and clerks of the fort, the factor from Rocky Mountain House and a trader from Fort Pitt. Father Lacombe had been invited but had declined in order to preside over his own festivities at St. Albert. The most unusual guest, excepting possibly Asher Mundy himself, was Robert Macklewaithe, who had made long journeys into the Arctic regions. There were no ladies present.

The sparsely furnished mess hall had a richness all its own with firelight and candlelight picking out the gay colours on the ceiling, the deep tapestry-like colours of Sam Mott's Indian pictures and the antlers, buffalo horns and guns decorating the fireplace.

The table was a sight. Down its length stretched a row of candles in brass holders, casting a glow on the polished wood and twinkling on the tin and pewter plates and cups. (The Company did not supply its posts with china or table-cloths.) Before the Chief Factor at the head of the table smoked a buffalo hump. But this was only one item of the feast. Before the place of each guest was some choice dish he was expected to serve to the company, beaver tongues, a dressed goose, a huge white-fish delicately browned in buffalo marrow, venison and at the end of the table farthest from the Chief Factor the rarest delicacy of all, a roast unborn whole buffalo calf. Basin-like dishes of mashed potatoes and turnips, the vegetables grown at the fort, were placed at convenient intervals. Whiskey also was served to everyone excepting only the Company's fifteen-year-old ward, who in the excitement of the occasion did not notice the omission.

At this primitive feast, served on a bare table in the half barbaric splendour of the mess hall, Asher's fringed and beaded tunic looked more suitable than the cloth jackets and white cravats of the other guests. He took his place before a dish of mouffle (moose nose) and, drawing out his hunting knife, set to work slicing and serving as neatly as the best of them.

"You see that man," said the trader from Fort Pitt in a low voice. He nodded towards the end of the table where Macklewaithe sat behind the buffalo calf. "Did you know he had been given a name in Cree, Nipoo-winikwao, which means Death-in-the-Face?"

"No," said Asher. "Why is he called that?"

"You can take your choice. Some say it means he has looked death in the face. Probably true. Its the meaning *he* inclines to. Others say he has a curse on him. He's the only survivor of his Arctic expedition. All the others died. That, to say the least, is unlucky," finished the trader. "For the others," he added drily.

This bit of information roused Asher's interest. When, in reply to a question, Macklewaithe began to talk about himself, Asher was his most attentive listener.

"I come of a military family," he began. "There have always been soldiers among us. I too was trained for the army and received my commission. But since the defeat of Napoleon Bonaparte there have been no great wars, nor is there likely to be one in my lifetime. A young man ambitious for honour must look elsewhere than to the battlefield.

"I went on an expedition to the Arctic Sea with Captain George Back who was later knighted for his efforts. That determined me to be an explorer. But as I do not willingly serve under another man and was desirous for fame on my own account, I sought and received a commission from the Hudson's Bay Company to explore in the Arctic regions. And so I led my own expedition."

"It was not a very fortunate one," commented the trader who sat by Asher.

"I do not agree with you, sir," said Captain Macklewaithe, looking directly at the man. "I returned with my maps and notes intact and the discovery of new regions to report to the Hudson's Bay Company. I shall conduct another expedition to the Arctic. But this time I hope to use a different type of man. The French *voyageur* may prove useful to the traders in Rupert's Land, but he has not the qualities for exploration in the Arctic."

Chief Factor Rowand was looking explosively red at his end of the table.

"I didn't invite the fellow here to make a speech," he muttered. He longed to tell Macklewaithe that if he did not know how to deal with *voyageurs,* he likely would not know how to deal with men of any type. But his position as host forbade quarrelling with a guest. So he banged on the table and in a voice that overrode all conversation announced: "Gentlemen, we will now rise and drink a toast to Her Majesty the Queen."

"When I travelled in those regions," said Macklewaithe after the toast was drunk, continuing his story for the benefit of those nearest him, "I constantly had the feeling that I had arrived at the ends of the earth and that the uttermost limits of terrestrial geography awaited my discovery."

"Are there furs there?" asked the trader.

"Furs in abundance, sir, as I have reported to the Company. But as a trader interested in buying and selling and making profits I fear you cannot understand the fascination this country holds for those few of us who are truly explorers. Do you realize, sir, that we aspire to reach the ultimate point, the Pole itself. The reward, I grant you, is not of the commercial order, but for us it is greater. It is fame."

One at least of his listeners, the youngest one, accepted him without question. "The ends of the earth!" How the phrase rang in Asher's imagination. Here was a man he would willingly follow to the ends of the earth.

After the company rose from the table and broke up into little groups lingering before the big fireplace and about the room, Asher approached Captain Macklewaithe. Encouraged by the after-dinner mood of the guests and his own enthusiasm, he asked the explorer to consider him as a recruit for his next Arctic expedition.

Macklewaithe looked him over sharply and asked him a number of practical questions. He asked him his age.

Asher answered truthfully that he would be sixteen that spring, which meant that he would really be entering upon his seventeenth year. Put that way it made him seem quite grown up. He told Macklewaithe frankly of his position at the fort.

"I have given a promise to Mr. Rowand not to leave without his permission. If you would speak to him, perhaps—"

"But are you not a ward of the Hudson's Bay Company?"

"Yes, sir, I am."

"Then I shall speak to Sir George Simpson about you. I know him well."

Asher was delighted. That would certainly free him. Macklewaithe told him he was wintering at forts farther north, but that the Arctic expedition would not be made up till the summer. In the meantime he would try to make an arrangement with the Governor to take Asher with him. He shook hands with Asher. He treated him like a man.

Presently Chief Factor Rowand and his guests joined the Christmas party in full swing in the Indian Hall. To this party had been invited every inhabitant of the fort, man, woman and child, as well as any who chose to come from the surrounding country. Indian women and their children squatted along the walls, while the more pretentious *bois-brulés* sat about on chairs and benches. The young people danced the Red River jig and Scotch reels to the tune of two fiddles, *two,* no less that kept very good time and managed to stay together in a remarkable fashion.

Asher, in the highest spirits after his interview with the explorer, was soon jigging about with a roguishly pretty Indian girl who gave him her full attention until a six-foot *voyageur* magnificent in red shirt, fringed sash and beaded moccasins swept her away from him. Asher was at first annoyed, but decided it would be ill-bred to start a row at a party, especially over such a small matter as a girl. Instead he retired to the side lines and looked superior. How little this crowd could imagine the glorious thoughts that filled his mind! The prospect of unbelievable adventure!

He talked for a while with Napoleon Boucher, hinting at his wonderful plans.

"So you have met the man called Death-in-the-Face. Tell me, how is his face? Like a spectre?"

"Of course not," said Asher indignantly. "Captain Macklewaithe has a countenance full of benevolence."

"Is it possible?" said Napoleon.

Asher noticed that Captain Macklewaithe had not come to the dance. In keeping with his new mood of superiority he himself left a little before the party broke up—but only a little before.

VI

During the month of January, Chief Factor Rowand gave some attention to the affairs of Asher Mundy and decided to send him to Fort Garry without waiting for the spring brigade. This was a grave decision which he made only after careful consideration. The boy was rest-less and discontented and, although Rowand trusted him to keep his promise during the winter, he could not help fearing that once the movement of brigades and hunting parties began in the spring, Asher would find some ingenious way of getting around it. Then, too, his disapproval of the influence Captain Macklewaithe had acquired over the boy at Christmas helped Rowand to make up his mind.

He sent for Napoleon Boucher and offered him the charge of a small, well-equipped expedition to go to Fort Garry. Winter travel across the prairie was usually made in relays. But in the case of this expedition, what-ever changes might be made in the other members of the party, Napoleon was to undertake to go the whole journey to Fort Garry and take Asher Mundy with him.

"You are an experienced *hivernant*," Rowand told Napoleon, "and even though Mundy is wintering for the first time he looks upon you as a friend and will give his best."

The Hudson's Bay Company was careful of its finan-ces, especially in the matter of wages. Rowand could not offer much for this exceptional and difficult expedi-tion. Even so, what he did offer was more than a *voy-ageur* could expect normally to earn in the winter. Napo-leon, after a little hesitation and some questions, willing-ly accepted.

Asher's consent, of course, was not necessary. Never-theless Rowand hoped to present the plan to him in such a way as to gain his good will and co-operation.

He was astonished and angry when Asher told him, quite politely, that after Captain Macklewaithe had spoken to Sir George Simpson about him, he expected to be released from his promise and allowed to join the Arctic expedition.

"Have you forgotten you have a father?" asked Rowand, whose voice when angry tended to rise like a rising gale. "You must know the Governor has no control over your future. How can you be so stupid! But I have not found you stupid in other matters so I must conclude that you have deliberately deceived Captain Macklewaithe."

Asher was silent. He had not deceived Macklewaithe. He was confused himself about his position. But how explain that to Rowand? Why bother?

This tiresome little interview took place in the Chief Factor's office and was interrupted by a clerk with the news that Father Lacombe had arrived at the fort on his way to St. Albert. He had to leave his horse because of the deep snow and was asking for snow-shoes to complete his journey.

"Of course I'll supply the snow-shoes, Mr. Rowand, but I thought you would want to be notified that Father Lacombe was here."

"Snow-shoes!" roared the Chief Factor, glad of an interruption. "Nonsense! Mundy, have a dog-team harnessed for Father Lacombe. And on the way stop at the kitchen and tell them to send up a pot of tea and some food."

Rowand went down to the gate and found the missionary, hollow-eyed from fatigue and starvation insisting, as a tired man will, that he must push on without delay.

"Alexis is sick. I was able to send him ahead. I must get home. My dear boy," he said to the clerk, "why do you not give me the snow-shoes and say nothing?"

"The dog-sled will get you there much faster," said Rowand. "Tomorrow you will thank me for this."

"You are a stubborn man," said the priest, following the Chief Factor into his house. "You remind me of myself."

In the office, while the missionary ate the lunch provided for him, Rowand talked to him about Asher Mundy and his plan to send him to Fort Garry.

"I like the lad, but he is headstrong and unmanageable, especially since he has chosen Macklewaithe for his hero."

"He wants to stay in the North West," commented Father Lacombe. "Most young men are the same."

"It is not as simple as that. There's the matter of his father's consent and a legacy to be settled. And now there is the hold Macklewaithe has gained over the boy's mind."

"Yes, indeed," agreed the priest vaguely. He was very tired and he wanted to be on his way.

"I like the boy," repeated Rowand. "He is too good to do a dog's work for that vain ambitious man. I'll send him to look after the team and sled. That will give you a chance to talk to him. Try, Father, to put him in a better frame of mind."

"But I have no influence with this boy," protested Father Lacombe. At the moment it seemed too much on top of everything else.

Asher, wearing a belted and hooded *capote* of heavy blanket cloth, came into the room to say the cariole was ready.

"Am I to drive it, Mr. Rowand?"

"Have you had the dogs out alone?"

"Once, sir. I don't think I'll have any trouble. I took great care to pick the best dogs."

"I'll have this young man, if you please," said Father Lacombe.

They went down to the gate where the cariole and four dogs were waiting. Father Lacombe, somewhat revived by the hot tea and food, stretched out in the cariole and drew the buffalo robes about him.

"Quel luxe!" he murmured wearily. "Merci, merci beaucoup."

Asher slung his snow-shoes across his back till they were away from the fort. He then put them on and ran along behind the cariole, ready, if the snow had drifted, to go ahead and break the trail. But the snow was sufficiently hard packed for the dogs and the trail to St. Albert was in good condition.

Father Lacombe slept all the way. When they arrived an hour later he awoke declaring himself greatly refreshed and led Asher into his house. He went immediately to Alexis who was tossing with fever on his bed and set about making him comfortable.

In the kitchen of the little house Asher built up the fire which was almost out and put on the kettle. It was

a little like old times at Sam Mott's back home, only
this house was poorer and tidier. Asher looked about,
found food and set the table. The priest, when he came
from tending the sick man, looked surprised and pleased.
The two sat down to supper.

Asher began questioning Father Lacombe about the
Cree language which he said he was learning. He tried
out words and phrases and then drew out of his pouch
a paper on which he had been trying to set down the
new sounds phonetically. Again the priest was pleasant-
ly surprised. It was somewhat in this way he had learned
Cree. He found himself giving Asher a little lesson on
the elements of Cree grammar and usage.

He recalled the things Rowand had told him about
this boy. Then he began to think of his own brother Gas-
pard who had run away to the North West and now
spent his life wandering the plains from Texas to the
Peace River. A wasted life, the priest feared. But Gas-
pard was a simple, happy-go-lucky soul. The boy beside
him he suspected was of a different temperament. He
would tire of the life that now seemed so desirable. In
a few years he would be a man, bitter with the sense of
his wasted talents.

As though his thoughts too had turned into another
channel Asher said suddenly:

"Why can't my father leave me alone! Why is he trying to make me go home!"

"You are not of age," said the priest. "You owe him
some obedience."

"Why does he want to make me do what I don't want to do?"

"Has he a career planned that you do not wish to follow?"

"No," said Asher uncertainly. "It's not exactly that." Then changing the subject suddenly as was his habit he asked the priest fiercely, "What would you have done if someone had left you a legacy requiring you to do something else when you wanted to be a missionary?"

The priest considered this involved question, then said firmly. "I should have given up the legacy."

"Oh," said Asher, taken aback. "I can't do that. I've spent some of it."

"You are speaking now of the legacy from Samuel Mott. Do you know its provisions?"

"Not precisely."

"But you think there is something?"

"I think he wanted me to go away and study to be an artist."

"And you do not wish to be an artist?"

"It's not exactly that," said Asher, floundering again. "But I don't want to have to leave this country now."

"Do you perhaps know what you want to do?"

"Yes," said Asher. He would not be caught short this time. "I want to be an Arctic explorer."

Just since Christmas, Father Lacombe wanted to say. Just since you met Macklewaithe whom Rowand calls a vain ambitious man and the Crees Nipoowinikwao which is Death-in-the-Face. But he feared he had already pressed his questions too hard and was antagonizing the boy. He sighed, realizing that he must leave these things unsaid. Instead he said: "M'sieu Rowand is a man of experience and he is your friend. Do not hesitate to take his good advice. To run away once," Father Lacombe shrugged, "yes, perhaps. But to keep on running away. That is not reasonable. You should go to Fort Garry and settle the matter of the legacy. You should see your father. Then it will be more suitable for you to take on a man's career."

After supper Asher went out to feed the dogs and tie them up for the night so that he would not have to run all over the settlement after them in the morning. They were good dogs. He had chosen well. Perhaps the Chief Factor would let him have them when he set out for Fort Garry. This thought brought more painful ones to his mind.

No one saw his point of view. No one understood that he did not want to wait till he was grown up to do things. Then it would be too late for him to enjoy his youth. Then he would be like *them*, careful, prudent, thinking, *reasonable*!

When he went into the house, Father Lacombe was still sitting by the table reading his breviary. Asher wished him good night politely. Then thinking something more was needed he said:

"Thank you, Père Lacombe, for the lesson in Cree and also," he added stiffly, "for your advice."

Father Lacombe smiled and then began to laugh like Sam Mott used to, less boisterously, but in the same warm, friendly tone.

"Don't feel badly that they send you to Fort Garry. I do not have worry for you. You will find what you want. But now you do not know what it is you want."

Wasn't that a queer thing to say, thought Asher, after he was in bed. Père Lacombe expressed himself a little oddly sometimes when he spoke in English. Could he really have meant that he, Asher Mundy, didn't know what he wanted?

7. The Bear

I

AT LAST THEY were on their way. It was good to be travelling even if it was in the wrong direction.

"You will travel like a prince," Rowand said. He had outfitted them with a sled and four-dog team to carry their camping equipment, personal baggage and the mail going to Fort Garry. They also had a cariole with a three-dog team carrying a very light load which they could ride in when they felt the need. Two Indians with the Christian names of James and John were accompanying them for at least half the way. Five sleds with their dog teams and men, the regular midwinter packet, were going with them as far as Fort Pitt.

Before he left, Asher gave his two horses to Cyprian Ouellette. He wanted to make some return for the hospitality and kindness he had received from that family. Rowand pointed out that he could not legally transfer the horses, especially as Asher had acquired them in a peculiar way from the Company's wardens. But he promised that Cyprian should be left in possession of them and he was confident Asher would be able to make the transfer legal when he arrived at Fort Garry.

Asher said goodbye to his friends at the fort. Mama Ouellette gave him a huge pair of deerskin mitts almost big enough to put his head in. Touched by her kindness he had kissed her and embraced and kissed Cyprian and all the children.

Rowand gave final definite instructions to Napoleon Boucher. He was under no circumstances to separate from Asher or trust him to anyone else. If by some mischance Napoleon fell ill or met with an accident he was to leave Asher with the factor of the nearest post. The factor would have instructions to cover the situation. Rowand did not foresee that the accident might happen to Asher. But of course no one could have foreseen the bear.

The Chief Factor and most of Fort Edmonton came to wish the winter brigade bon voyage. Some followed them through the gates to watch them descend to the river and spread out in single file along the frozen Saskatchewan. They were off!

Napoleon Boucher and his party travelled prosperously in this company. The weather was clear, men and dogs fresh. They made good time. At night they camped at some spot along the bank where there was evergreen for their beds and plenty of firewood. They slept in a big circle, feet toward the camp fire, wrapped in their *capotes* and buffalo robes, a rampart of snow scraped from the camping spot their only wall, without roof or tent although the temperature was far below zero.

Asher had hardly believed Joe Labrie when he had told him this was the mode of winter travel in Rupert's Land. Now he was experiencing it himself. When the men told stories around the camp fire he could follow their rough racy French which he had not understood when he first travelled with the *voyageurs* from Fort William. So much he had gained from the months spent in the North West.

Fort Pitt, when they reached it, proved almost too crowded for comfort. The brigade from Norway House had arrived about the same time. There was not only the problem of housing but also of feeding so many extra people in the winter season. The two brigades exchanged their mail and goods, then without prolonging their stay, each started homeward.

From this point Napoleon and his party would travel alone to Fort Carlton. He had expected to get fresh supplies of food at Fort Pitt. But the factor suggested that he make use of a cache of food which had been built and stocked for the trappers and so far had not been needed. This cache Napoleon would find about two days' travel in the direction he was going.

It was strange at first to be without the lively company they had grown used to. But after the first night they seemed to draw together, the two Indians, James and John, Napoleon, Asher and the dogs, a little band of living creatures united against the cold and the vast, lonely country. They travelled in this fashion two days until they came to the food cache and met the bear.

He was an old bear. The natural course of his life had been broken and he was uneasy and bad-tempered. He should have been tucked away in some cranny, fat and cosy, for the winter. But during the past summer he had not grown fat—at least not fat enough. Now he was forced by hunger to leave his den and venture out into the cold and snow where there was little he cared to eat.

He had found the cache which had been built strongly of logs, but against lesser animals than him, for he was a big bear. Old and failing as he was, he had broken down a corner of the cache and got in at the pemmican. The place was littered with the stuff he had pulled out and strewn about. Once he had driven off wolves. Now he lived inside the cache.

Napoleon came up the slope on which the cache had been built, with Asher behind him. He gave an exclamation of dismay when he saw the mess. Then the bear rose up before him as suddenly as if he had come out of the ground, and so close that the *voyageur* did not have a chance to use his gun. With a low rumbling growl the beast stretched out a huge paw and knocked the astonished Napoleon flat. Indeed the cry he let out as he fell was as much surprise as fear.

Asher, whose gun was on the sled, stopped short. He could hear the Indians running. They were hunters; they would know what to do. The terror of the country which he had felt before paralysed him. Must he for a second time watch helplessly while a friend died? Was he going to lose Napoleon too? Fear turned to white rage. Yanking his sash loose he threw off his heavy encumbering *capote* and unsheathed his hunting knife. Then with a yell he sprang on the bear. He landed full on the creature's back and drove the knife with all his strength into the neck. He hit instinctively and blindly, but felt the knife sink in, in, right up to the hilt.

The bear reared, while Asher clung to his back as to a horse. He dug his knees in and with both hands clutched the coarse heavy fur. He had a mad idea that if he could hold on he was safe. The great paw came round in a frantic convulsive movement, caught him and tore his left arm from shoulder to wrist. He fell back, but by then Napoleon had rolled out of the bear's reach. Asher sprang to safety with a leap that would have done credit to a jack rabbit, that indeed would not have disgraced a kangaroo. The Indians reached the spot and from two sides took deadly accurate aim and sent their bullets into the bear.

It was a scene of confusion. The great animal, even with Asher's knife in his back and two bullets in his head, came on to the attack. But whom was he to attack? His enemies were all around him. Napoleon had retrieved his gun and sent another shot into him. By this time the Indians had reloaded and returned for the kill. The bear soon lay quiet on the churned and blood-stained snow.

But even after his growls and roars ceased the shouts of the men continued. To come upon a bear in winter! To have to attack it on foot! An extraordinary thing. Bears throughout the North West had a reputation above all other animals for strength and tenacity of life. They were rarely hunted except on horseback and by a group.

"Ashair, what has happened to you?" said Napoleon. Asher was sitting on the snow, winded.

"It got me in the arm," he said.

"Oh, mon Dieu!" gasped Napoleon. The sight sobered him. "Where is your *capote*?" He picked it up and wrapped it round the boy. "Come," he said. "We'll get a fire made and look after this."

II

They returned to the sleds and while the Indians got the fire going Napoleon slit the sleeve of Asher's buckskin shirt. Though torn by the bear's claws, the sleeve had protected the flesh to the middle of the upper arm. There three claw marks began, one very deep almost to the bone and extending over the elbow almost to the wrist. They were nasty, ragged-looking wounds but did not bleed excessively.

Napoleon washed the arm first with snow, then with hot water after the fire was started. He bound it with a clean woollen sash from his own baggage. It was the best he could do. He knew there were herbs which would keep a wound from festering. One of the Indians said that if it were summer time he could find these plants. But as it was, their best hope for remedies was to find an Indian camp or better still reach Fort Carlton as quickly as possible.

Their first task was to skin the bear and cut themselves some meat from its carcase. This double duty James and John carried out with praiseworthy speed. The skin, though large, was not in prime condition and the meat was unbelievably tough. The only good eating was in the marrow bones.

"The old fellow has given us plenty of trouble and now he gives us indigestion," commented Napoleon struggling with his portion. Nevertheless they needed the meat as all the food in the cache had been eaten or spoilt. Only the dogs, who were given their share, enjoyed the meal.

James and John bundled up the bloody, stiffening bearskin and made a separate parcel of the four paws. Bear claws were an ornament of great distinction among the Indians, signifying courage and prowess. In this case it is true the honour of killing the bear had to be divided four ways, with the greatest honour going to Asher. Even the hunters with their guns could not have saved Napoleon from a horrible mauling, if indeed they could have rescued him alive.

Within two hours they had broken camp and were on their way, Asher because of his wound riding in the cariole. One day passed, two days passed. Napoleon despaired of doing anything in a medical way for Asher. The improvised bandage was soaked with blood and stuck to the wound. The skin of the arm looked inflamed and swollen; the claw marks were filling with pus. Asher assured him cheerfully that his arm was only moderately uncomfortable. Napoleon was careful not to let him know his own concern. He sharply stopped the Indians when they started to give an opinion on the possible outcome.

Three days passed. Napoleon drove the men and dogs even more relentlessly than he had Asher and Sam Mott on the way to Fort Sault Ste. Marie. And as on that occasion he did not spare himself.

He went ahead with one Indian and the four-dog team. Asher in the cariole and the second Indian followed. The uncanny instinct of the leading dog and the skilled observation of the Indian found trails even in this apparently trackless wasteland. During the winter months Indian trappers and mail packets had made their way between Fort Pitt and Fort Carlton. Napoleon depended on the Indians to find the trail, the leading dog to hold it, while he used time and speed to the best advantage.

He allowed only four hours for sleep. They travelled mostly at night. Along the open path of the river or across stretches of country bare of trees the clear nights provided all the light they needed, while the daylight hours were short and the glare of the sun on the snow often blinding. Four, sometimes five stops were allowed for hot tea and food. This indulgence was really for Asher to give him a chance to get thoroughly warmed and to whip up the circulation after hours of inactivity in the cariole.

The weather favoured them. It was, Napoleon decided on the morning of the fourth day, too favourable. The windlessness, the first faint, very faint film of vapour tempering the glare of the sun were signs of a storm. They dare not risk another night in the open. But if the storm caught them in the afternoon they could not hope to reach the fort. They might have to remain in a snow camp for several days and Napoleon feared the affect this hardship and further neglect might have on Asher's festering arm. That day he allowed only one stop.

Asher stumbled out of the sled and began scooping snow into the kettle. He had been dozing, dreaming uneasily that he was again with the canoe brigade, that he was cold and wet and Napoleon was shouting, "Marche! marche!" which was a command for dogs and not for men.

"I'll run alongside for a while," he said. "It's tiresome riding wrapped up like a papoose."

"No, no," said Napoleon, not liking the look of Asher's flushed cheeks and feverish eyes. "You are in bad condition. You ride in the cariole."

"Nonsense. My arm feels better. Fix a sling for it, Nap. I'll run alongside for a while."

"You will ride in the cariole," ordered Napoleon. "I command it. There is a storm coming and we cannot lose time."

"Oh, all right, all right," said Asher irritably. "I know you're in charge. But you needn't treat me like a child. A storm is coming—" he mimicked.

"Listen to the boy," cried the much-tried Napoleon. "Sainte Vierge! He doesn't believe a storm is coming. You'll see."

Napoleon marshalled his little force for the last lap. Only a few more hours. Nothing must happen. The weather must hold. They must have no accident, no delay.

"If we arrive safely," he prayed, "I'll light candles of thanksgiving in the Church of St. Boniface."

It is to be hoped he remembered this pious vow because his prayer was answered. Late in the afternoon they arrived at Fort Carlton ahead of the storm.

III

Their first greeting was a rough one. As they came into the stockade the dogs of the fort rushed out at their teams. Soon they were all rolling about in a tangle of harness, fur and upset sleds. The men shouted and beat and yanked and kicked. Asher tried to do his share but soon gave up. He was useless. His arm was more painful and he felt more unwell than he cared to admit even to himself. When order was restored he went into the fort with the others, cradling his injured left arm in his right.

The building was not as good as Fort Pitt and certainly not nearly as fine as Fort Edmonton. After days in the open Asher could scarcely bear to breathe the air inside, thick and stale with a mixture of unpleasant smells.

The factor greeted them kindly and told them the fort was in a bad way. A band of Indians camped beside them was stricken with measles. The fort's best Indian hunter had died of it. They were short of supplies and the hunting this winter was unusually poor. Had they seen any game?

Napoleon had to admit that, apart from a big old bear which they had killed, they had seen no game.

The factor said he could give the young man with the injured arm good news. They had a doctor with them, who had come from Fort Garry. He would attend to him.

Mr. Finlay, the surgeon, proved to be a sandy-haired young man with an Edinburgh accent. He cut away the crude bandaging without comment and examined Asher's arm carefully. The factor and his clerk, an Indian attached to the fort, James and John and Napoleon, all watched. The gashes from the bear's claws were festering, the flesh along the edges discoloured and bits of the bandage caked with blood stuck in the wounds. Napoleon watched the doctor's face but it told him nothing.

Mr. Finlay was thinking: Too bad this happens when I have no nitrate of silver left. It will have to be actual cautery, the quickest and cleanest method, but red-hot iron terrifies the patient. Aloud he said evenly: "I can save the arm. It will have to be cauterized."

"Just what is that, sir?" asked Asher politely. He was greatly frightened.

"Hot iron, my lad."

"Red-hot?"

"It's not as bad as it sounds."

"Thank you," said Asher still very politely. "But that will not be necessary. If you will have the kindness to put on fresh bandages and fix me with a sling it will heal itself."

"Ashair, I implore you," burst out Napoleon. But Asher continued, his voice rising with determination.

"I will never consent to having my arm cut off."

"I am not going to cut it off," said the doctor patiently. "You have my word on it. But look at it. You see. I must clean it first. Then I'll bandage it and give you a sling. Take him into the other room," he said to the factor. "Remove his shirt and give him a double dram of whiskey."

"This is good luck," Napoleon assured him as they got him ready. "A real surgeon. Those fellows know what they're doing."

The factor handed him the mug of whiskey. "I take it you're not used to spirits. Don't drink it too fast, but drink it all."

Asher did as he was told. The drink burnt in his throat in a peculiar but not unpleasant way. It warmed him inside. His arm no longer pained him and presently a comfortable feeling of indifference came over him. If the doctor wanted to treat his injured arm, he didn't mind.

They returned to the main room where the doctor had everything ready and their audience, James and John and the third Indian, awaited them. The factor remained to assist the doctor. The clerk might have tactfully withdrawn, but since one more or less wasn't going to matter, he stayed too. Asher sat by the table and Napoleon stood beside him.

"Don't watch me," the doctor told him. "Look elsewhere and think how good it will be to have your left arm for the rest of your life."

"You'd better talk to me," Asher said to Napoleon.

"Certainly," he replied agreeably. "In French or English."

"French. I'll have to think harder."

So they discussed the blizzard. Napoleon said it would come that night. Asher asked him how he knew.

The doctor sponged the wounds, removed bits of cloth, trimmed away the dead tissue with a sharp razor. Then the factor handed him the iron heated to a dull red and he applied it to the wounds.

Asher reared out of the chair, but Napoleon's hands on his shoulders forced him down. The factor held the arm steady. Time whirled round, settled down to pain and stopped—nothing but pain, startling pain that went on endlessly. It didn't seem possible that anything so shocking could go on and on. Asher drew his breath in through his clenched teeth, but he did not cry out. He could not. The pain had taken away his voice. He did not speak even when the others began to speak and Napoleon said: "Voilà, c'est fini."

The doctor bandaged the arm and bound it in a splint, saying that the sling must wait for a day or two. The factor thought it proper to congratulate him upon his performance. The three Indians exchanged brief words in their own language. The white boy had stood the ordeal well. Asher sat white and shaken. Then suddenly he stepped over to the fireplace and deposited his drink of whiskey in the ashes.

"A pity," said Napoleon gently. "A great waste. Perhaps we should have given it to him after."

"No," said the doctor. "The drink served its purpose. It might be well to help your young friend to bed. I'll come in later to see him."

8. Ghost Dancers in the Sky

I

THE STORM DIRELY foretold by Napoleon swept down on them. Wind, cold, and the air filled with whirling snow turned the out-of-doors into a raging white inferno. The wretched plague-infected Indian camp became a haven of safety and the fort a most desirable spot. For two days no one ventured out. The doctor wrote his report, recording his failure to stop the epidemic among the Indians and his success in cauterizing an infected arm, in the same detached scientific manner. Napoleon lounged before the fire and Asher moved about restlessly. The roar of the wind excited him. It swept round

134

and over the fort and shook it till, sturdily built as it was, it creaked under the strain. Asher melted a hole on the frosted window-pane and peered out. There was nothing to see but a tiny glimpse of whirling driving snow.

"If we had been caught in that we would all have died," he said.

"Oh, no," said Napoleon. "Those who travel with Napoleon Boucher do not die even in a blizzard."

"What would you have done?"

"We would wrap ourselves in our blankets and robes and use the sleds as shelter. When the snow drifts over you are in a little hole out of the wind. But you need a little fire or smudge. If there is no wood, buffalo dung will do. And that may be found by scraping below the snow. It is even possible to boil some tea. But frankly it is not pleasant. Even beasts wouldn't enjoy such accommodations."

"But what if there were no fuel of any kind?"

Napoleon shrugged.

"That would be unfortunate."

"We're better off here."

"But yes, naturally."

The measles epidemic had run its course and the doctor wished to return to Fort Garry. He asked to join Napoleon and his party.

"You are welcome," said Napoleon promptly. "You pass your first winter in the country? So. Nevertheless you are welcome. But you must understand my position. You are first time an *hivernant*. Asher Mundy is first

time *hivernant*. Unless we find someone else we will all
be here till spring. Still you are welcome."

James and John were not going any farther. The
country ahead was not their country and their undertaking had been to stay with the party only as far as
Fort Carlton. But the Indian at the fort, Young Beaver,
came from the Red River. He was the fort's second
hunter, recommended by the factor who was willing to
let him go when he found James and John would take
his place.

"I think you get the best of this bargain, M. le Facteur," said Napoleon.

"You have the doctor," the factor pointed out. "Besides, if game is scarce it will be easier to provide for
four than five."

They left Fort Carlton and the Saskatchewan. They
crossed the South Saskatchewan and still heading south
and east came out on the open plains where the wind
had carved the snow into curled waves with wisps of fine
snow blowing off the crests. There was nothing to see
to the horizon but an occasional dark blur like an island
which marked a bluff of little trees. They drove towards
one of these whenever they needed a fire.

The factor had provided them with pemmican and
flour, but not enough for the whole journey. Plainsmen
always expected to supply themselves by hunting and
when, as sometimes happened in winter, the game failed, they starved. Hunger soon made a fifth member of
their party. It followed at their heels like a shadowy

animal and sat with them at their meals when Napoleon doled out their soupy ration of pemmican and flour cooked in water. It haunted them in sleep. It never let them forget its presence.

Each lived with hunger after his own fashion. The doctor took the scientific view and noted that with a fire to warm them and sleep at intervals, with a turn in the cariole from time to time, they were able on their snowshoes to keep up with the dogs hour after hour, day after day, with never one full meal. The Indian bore hunger stoically; he had suffered it before. Napoleon entertained them at meals with stories of men reduced to eating their dogs and even gnawing their moccasin laces and rawhide whips, although he stopped short of the darker tales of cannibalism. His intention was only to cheer them up by showing that they were not so badly off. Asher lost weight faster than the men and became very silent. No one complained.

Ah, it was a bleak country! Nothing lived or moved in it except themselves. Even the animals that should have provided them with food were gone. There was nothing to look at but the sky. The sky was everywhere and at night it was beautiful. The northern lights flashed across it, spreading whitely to the horizon or gathering into the zenith of the heavens, where the light hung in showers and prisms of the most delicate colours. Sometimes the movement was slow like water gradually flooding the sky. Sometimes the light swept almost playfully like veils rippling and tossing through the air. Ghost dancers, the spirits of the dead, the Indians said.

When I die, thought Asher, would I want to run about the sky waving banners of light? I don't think so. Something more like the Vikings' heaven. That's better. A great hall and feasting, food, food. I can't forget I'm hungry even for a minute. Not even when I'm asleep. I'd rather have the pain in my arm again than this.

He looked at the little band spread out in line, the dogs, the two sleds, his three companions. Napoleon waved to him and gave a great sweeping gesture with his arm drawing his attention again to the heavens.

Had anyone ever painted the Aurora Borealis? Would it be possible? Could you paint light? Sam had said that if you studied with a good master you learned all he knew and then you added to it. You could paint subjects only you yourself had thought of. Sam had been an explorer as well as an artist. More an explorer than an artist, hadn't he? He'd surely approve of Asher's wanting to be an explorer.

Only once since they had left Fort Edmonton did he and Napoleon speak of Captain Macklewaithe and then only briefly and indirectly.

"Could the Arctic regions get any colder than this?" Asher asked after they had pitched camp because of piercing wind and driving snow that cut their toughened faces like glass splinters. The sleds were unpacked and up-ended, with a robe stretched between them to shelter them while they dug a pit in the snow for their camp and fire.

"I don't know," said Napoleon. "I've never been there." Then thinking to encourage a little conversation with the

boy he asked. "Do you still want to go with Death-in-
the-Face to look for the North Pole?"

"Yes," said Asher. "It would be worth starving to
find the North Pole; it's not worth it just to reach Fort
Garry."

Napoleon for once had nothing to say.

That night Sam Mott visited him in a dream. Asher
saw him quite clearly, standing close to him, looking as
he had before his illness, strong and vigorous with the
prairie wind blowing in his beard. His face wore an
expression of anger such as Asher had never seen before.
Samuel Mott reached out and touched Asher's right
hand which burst into flame. The pain was excrucia-
ting. Asher woke with a shriek that roused his three
companions. They slept close together for warmth,
the doctor and Asher in the middle, the hardier *voyageur*
and Indian on either side of them.

"Build up the fire," ordered the doctor, and deftly and
quickly removed the bandaging from Asher's wounded
arm.

"Sam Mott stood there in my dream," said Asher, "and
set my hand afire."

The doctor finished his examination.

"The arm is healing cleanly. You may have rolled on
it in your sleep and hurt yourself."

"It was my right hand that was afire," stated Asher.

"There's naught wrong with your right hand," said
the doctor in his most positive Scottish tone. He looked

at Asher curiously. "We are all suffering from hunger, lad. It may be you have a touch of delirium."

Asher shook his head. "I saw him. Why did he bring fire?" he asked Napoleon. "Did he come from hell?"

"A soul cannot come from hell," replied Napoleon. "It was the fire of purgatory, perhaps."

"But Sam was a Protestant. He couldn't go to purgatory."

"In the other life," countered Napoleon, "it may be that matters are arranged differently."

"This is uncouth superstition," interrupted the doctor, who was a rationalist. "I'm going to sleep and I would advise you to do likewise and save your strength."

Young Beaver who had not understood much of the conversation had already rolled himself in his blanket.

"When Indian boys are about your age," said Napoleon, ignoring the doctor, "they submit themselves to painful ceremonies of initiation. Then after fasting they receive a dream. Perhaps you have had such an experience."

"How could I?" asked Asher impatiently. "I am not an Indian."

"I have known white men to submit to the initiation. But I do not know if they receive the dream. In it the Indian discovers his totem. Did the dream have anything to do with your future?"

Asher pulled the blankets about him, suddenly cold. "Sam Mott wanted me to be an artist like him. He left me his money to go to some foreign country like Italy and learn to paint portraits."

"Is that what it says in his will?" asked Napoleon curiously. He had heard various stories about Asher Mundy's inheritance.

"I have not seen the will. But he spoke of it."

Napoleon talked for a while about Indian belief in dreams and totems, about messages from the dead and such matters. At last his remarks trailed off and with a comfortable grunt or two he fell asleep.

Asher remained awake, huddled in his blankets, brooding over his dream. His mind, like a dog with something new, sniffed all around it; like a hand with a strange object, felt it all over. His mind found it a very solid experience. He was satisfied that the dream, though a dream, was real. He had seen Sam Mott.

When the sky grew bright with morning he was still awake. Napoleon was rousing them for another day, for what under happier circumstances would have been breakfast.

II

This day was like all the others. They continued their endless march; they suffered from hunger. Napoleon changed his efforts to cheer them. Instead of telling them horrible stories of the last stages of starvation he said that this could not go on forever. Sooner or later they were sure to find game. He believed it would be soon. But this happy thought did not immediately produce a buffalo.

No reference was made to Asher's dream, since he himself did not mention it. All day words and phrases of an old story ran through his mind like a tune: "And took his journey into a far country and there wasted his substance with riotous living—took his journey into a far country—his journey into a far country—and after he had spent all there arose a mighty famine in that land; and he began to be in want—there arose a mighty famine in that land."

He knew the Bible story. He knew how it ended. A pretty poor ending, he had always thought. The boy going home like that. He would not be so scornful in the future. He knew the decision he had come to and he knew what he would do when he came to Fort Garry.

That afternoon Young Beaver shot a rabbit. It was a small kill for a buffalo hunter, but no one offered the slightest criticism and everyone showed the greatest interest. Young Beaver skinned the little animal carefully. The doctor quartered it with precision. Napoleon cooked it, throwing in a great many ideas (he had little else to add) about the exact amount of water that would give the best concentration of juices and the exact length of time that would produce the best texture in the meat.

Asher, who had made the fire, sat watching the pot with hungry eyes. When the portions were served he wolfed his so ravenously that Napoleon protested:

"Eat it slowly and it will seem like more."

Ashamed of his voracity Asher began to pick and chew at the little that was left. Young Beaver had devoured his share almost at a gulp and was squatting, impassively, by the fire, his arms crossed over his belly as though in some cowlike way he was able to chew it again.

Napoleon waved a leg bone ("It will freeze if you don't eat it fast," warned Asher) and conversed with the doctor.

"You may not believe me," he said, "but I have eaten meat that has stood for some time and had a bad smell. That meat was good to eat, tender and of delicious flavour. Can you believe that?"

"Certainly," said the doctor. "In the Old Country meat is always hung till it is tender. It is only in this savage country that meat is eaten as soon as it is killed."

"Is it possible?" said Napoleon astonished.

Asher had finished his share and still felt hungry. But in a short time he began to feel satisfied and comfortable and this wonderful feeling continued for several hours.

Dim blue hills cut off the horizon as they entered the Qu'Appelle Valley. This was a beautiful country, beloved by all the prairie people who told many legends concerning it. But at this season it was as bleak and dreary as the rest of the world. Here they met a band of Crees who were also starving, but who had just had news from their scouts of a herd of buffalo.

Napoleon and Young Beaver went with the hunting party. The doctor and Asher, who were too weak for the rigours of the hunt, were given shelter in one of the lodges. Here they watched the women with few words and desperate optimism building up their fire and setting water to boil in their empty cooking-pot. In spite of the warmth of the smoky, smelly lodge it was a comfortless day. It was easier to endure hunger when in motion than when sitting still. Also it was humiliating to be left behind with the women. Not that that mattered much. Hunger left no room for pride or fine feelings.

Late in the day the hunters returned, dragging their crudely butchered carcasses. That night everyone feasted, even the dogs. The white men, knowing that they might be sick if they gorged after their long fast, ate heartily but prudently. The Indians ate till they stretched their skins and without any ill effects whatever.

For two days after they parted from the Crees, Napoleon and his party enjoyed full meals. Then they were on starvation rations again. But it did not seem to matter now. They had reached the Assiniboine River whose course led to their destination. They had only to survive a little longer. On the eighteenth day from Fort Carlton they arrived at Upper Fort Garry, weak but triumphant. Their dogs were uneaten and their moccasin laces unchewed. The worst had not happened to them.

They wasted no time but went directly to the Chief Factor's house and pounded on his kitchen door. It was a beautiful kitchen, warm and full of the smell of good food. The cook took in the situation at a glance and immediately began preparing a meal.

Mr. Christie himself came down when he heard they were there, greeted them and showed concern about Asher's arm which was still in a sling. Later, after they had eaten, he sent word that they were to be served a measure of rum in view of the exceptional hardships they had undergone. Remembering uncomfortably his drink at Fort Carlton, Asher refused his share which was given to the cook. Mr. Christie had also added to his message a request that Mr. Finlay the surgeon join him in his sitting-room.

When he and the doctor were seated over their rum, Mr. Christie came straight to the point.

"I am shocked at the boy's appearance, Mr. Finlay. Tell me frankly, as a doctor, is he in consumption?"

Mr. Finlay gave this idea thoughtful consideration. "I do not think so," he said at last. "I cannot recall a case of consumption that was not accompanied by a cough. Asher Mundy has no cough. In my opinion there is nothing wrong with him that a week's good eating won't cure."

"You will understand my concern when I tell you that Mr. Mundy, the boy's father, is here and presently I must send him to him."

"I beg your pardon," said the doctor. "Did I understand you to say that the boy's father is here, in Fort Garry?"

"Yes, he came by way of St. Paul in the American territory. He expected to find his son at Fort Garry. As you may imagine it was a delicate matter explaining that young Mundy had given us the slip. But I gave him the strongest assurance his son was at Fort Edmonton well taken care of and would be sent east with the spring brigade. Now I find he has been on the prairie for weeks. He arrives here skin and bone with a wounded arm into the bargain. How did he get that injury?"

"Fighting a bear."

The Chief Factor groaned. "What was Rowand thinking of to send him off in the winter? I have a long letter of explanation here, but I still think he was ill-advised."

"It may be for the best," said the doctor. "The boy is here. His father is here to take charge of him. Isn't that what everyone wanted? What induced Mr. Mundy to make such a trip in winter time?"

"There is a railway to St. Paul. But the journey up the Red River trail must have been pretty rugged."

"Is he here with you?"

"I'm sorry to say he isn't. I'd like to keep an eye on him. He is at the Riverman's House in the settlement. These journalists. Busybodies. They must poke their noses into everything. This is a hunting country, as you know, Mr. Finlay, and the Company doesn't like journalists. Talk of nothing but settlers, farming, railways. Spoil everything."

Mr. Christie poured the doctor more rum.

"I had a talk with this Mundy right here just the way I'm talking to you. 'This boy of yours,' I said, 'is almost of an age to be on his own. Why are you taking so much trouble to fetch him home?' 'He is my eldest son,' he told me. 'And I had great hopes for him. I would like him to choose a proper occupation. I cannot bear to have him fall into lawless and abandoned ways.' 'This is a

hunting country, Mr. Mundy,' I said, 'but it is not a lawless country.' Then I told him something about the
Hudson's Bay Company. I think, Mr. Finlay, I did a
stroke of business for us. I said, 'Your son is in this country and if he is like most young men he won't want to
leave it. Let him become an employee of the H.B.C. If
he has ability he can find an honourable and profitable
career.' I may say Mr. Mundy is a reasonable and intelligent man, even though a journalist. 'If that is what my
son has in mind to do,' he said, 'I'll give my consent.' "

"Then everything seems to be ending happily," said the
doctor.

"Perhaps you are right, Mr. Finlay. I regret the boy's
appearance. It does not speak well for our care of him.
But I suppose nothing can be done now."

Warmed by the Hudson's Bay Company's rum, the
doctor allowed himself a slow smile.

"I could shave him," he said. "I warrant he'd make a
fair appearance with the down removed and his hair
trimmed. It would not be the first time one of my pro-
fession turned to barbering."

The Chief Factor accepted this suggestion enthu-
siastically. They both went to the kitchen where Asher
was induced to submit to being shaved and having his
hair cut. A cauldron of water was set to heat and he
was encouraged to give himself a thorough scrubbing,
although bathing in the winter time was almost unheard
of in Rupert's Land. When he put on his fringed and
beaded Indian shirt all agreed he looked quite present-
able. On his own suggestion he discarded the sling.

With the good wishes of the doctor, the Chief Factor, the cook and Young Beaver, Asher set out with Napoleon for the Riverman's House. There Napoleon spoke vaguely of affairs elsewhere and left Asher who went in to meet his father alone.

9. How It All Ended

WHEN HIS SON came into the room where he was, Josiah
Mundy looked up and, seeing a tall gaunt young man
wearing a magnificent shirt, an expression of utter be-
wilderment came into his face. This expression in turn
affected Asher. He saw it and, although he did not understand its cause, was strangely moved. His father
seemed older and not as tall as he had remembered.
In a flash it occurred to him that his father had come
a long way and was alone in a strange country and not
very sure of himself. He felt sympathy for him and this
was a feeling he had never had before.

On an impulse, going over to him he put his arm about
his shoulders as he would have with Cyprian or Napo-

leon if he met them after an absence, saying some foolish, meaningless thing like: "Pa, why Pa, how did you
come here?"

He felt his father's arm about him, holding him tight,
inadvertently hurting his injured arm, and heard his
father's voice repeating rather shakily:

"Asher, my boy, my boy."

Of course Josiah Mundy had been startled to discover
his son had grown up, but he quickly realized that this
was natural and to be expected. It was Asher who was
most deeply surprised. His father had come so far to
find him and now greeted him with unexpected affection,
no scolding, no reproaches, not a single harsh word.
Something extraordinary was happening and he did not
understand it.

They were not alone for long. The Riverman's House
was a gathering place for *voyageurs*, brigade men and
winterers stranded in the Red River settlement till
spring. Napoleon joined them and between them he
and Asher told the story of the bear in a mixture of
French and English.

Napoleon generously and gratefully made it Asher's
story. It was a horrid experience to find oneself under-
neath an infuriated bear, the listeners agreed, and one
none of them would care to have. But to attack a bear
with a knife, that was something remarkable. And to
carry the scars for the rest of one's life to prove it, that
was an achievement worth something.

"The arm is still bandaged," Asher said casually because he knew they were looking at it curiously, although

they were too polite in the presence of his father to ask him to show it. The showing of scars was properly part of such a story. Asher remembered Sam Mott saying the Indians always wanted scars included in their portraits, even the ones in unpaintable places.

"Of course," Asher explained to his father, "I couldn't have killed the bear by myself with only a knife. The others helped. There were four of us."

What would his father think of all this boasting? But when he turned to make this explanation he found that Josiah Mundy's eyes were shining and his face as eager as any of the other listeners.

Later the company tactfully left Asher and his father alone, and the two of them had a serious conversation about his future.

"Mr. Christie seemed sure you want to remain in this country. He has offered you employment with the Hudson's Bay Company. I suppose that is what you want to do."

"Why no, Pa," said Asher surprised. "I have never wanted to be a trader."

At this point Josiah Mundy might well have taken a firm tone and pointed out his son's well-known faults of waywardness and wilfulness. But he was secretly pleased because he did not want Asher to join the Hudson's Bay Company. So instead he merely asked levelly, "And then?" and waited.

"I have decided," said Asher, "to go abroad and study to be an artist. It is what Sam Mott wanted me to do. He left money for it."

"Yes," said Josiah Mundy immediately interested. "He has that in the will."

"You have seen the will?" asked his son eagerly. "Did he say that was what I should do?"

"He did not make it an absolute condition, but he recommended it."

"It is what he wanted," said Asher.

Some day, he thought, I'll come back to this country. I'll go through the mountains. I'll paint the Indians that Sam Mott did not live to find. But this was something he could not tell anyone yet, not even his father. So he spoke of practical things.

"It is what he wanted," Asher repeated. "He said Italy. I know that's a long way off, across the ocean. I reckon I'll need a guide to get there. Do you know any gentleman, Pa, with whom I could travel to that country?"

"It could be arranged," said Josiah thoughtfully. "I might even go myself." The journalist in him seized on the idea. "That's what we'll do. I'll go with you to Italy and help you find a good drawing master or school or whatever is suitable. The journey will give me articles for the paper that will last for a twelve-month."

"Sounds fine," said Asher amiably.

"Asher," said his father, "I am very pleased with your decision. Very pleased with you indeed."

And of all the surprises that day had brought forth this was the most surprising. His father had never said anything like that to him before.

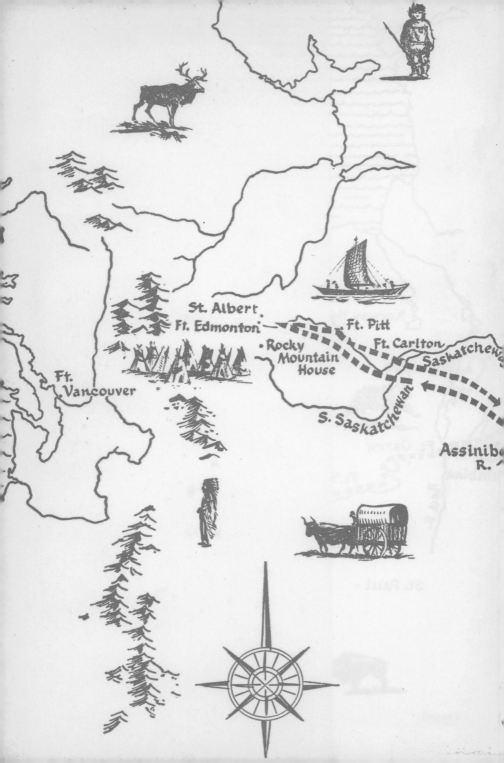

St. Albert
Ft. Edmonton
Ft. Pitt
Ft. Carlton
Rocky
Mountain
House
Saskatchewan
Ft.
Vancouver
S. Saskatchewan
Assiniboine
R.